# JUNGLE TALES

Airship 27 Productions

™

Jungle Tales-Volume 3

Published by Airship 27 Productions
www.airship27hangar.com

Interior llustrations © 2024 John Gallagher
Cover illustration © 2024 Ted Hammond

Managing Editor: Ron Fortier
Associate Editor: Jaime Ramos
Promotions Manager: Michael Vance
Production designer: Rob Davis

ISBN: 978-1-953589-84-2

Printed in the United States of America

10 9 8 7 6 5 4 3 2 1

# JUNGLE TALES
## Volume Three
### (FEATURING KI-GOR, JUNGLE LORD)

# THE LOST CITY

### By Curtis Fernlund

Belgian Congo
Leopoldville Province
Africa
1932

"**W**hat new hell is this, then?"

"It's called stew, George. Shut up and eat it."

"Bloody hell…"

William Bennet smirked, shaking his head as he listened to his colleague grumble and grouse. He'd learned over the past few weeks, his new friend from the *Empire Club* didn't seem to be happy unless he was complaining about something. First it was the size and condition of his cabin on the old ship, *Arundel Castle* sailing from the *Royal Albert Docks* at Liverpool on the Union-Castle Line to the port city of Banana at the mouth of the Congo River in West Africa. All through that long journey it was the food, the weather, the rough seas; a never-ending list of complaints, whatever caught his mood at the time. And when they finally hit the African coast after that lengthy sea voyage his attention shifted to the poor, crowded accommodations in the city, and the prices of supplies they needed and the quality of the porters and the guide to lead them deeper into the jungles of the Belgian-ruled Congo; the heat, the humidity, the rain, the insects, on and on. It never seemed to stop.

But in truth, George Saunders III was not such a bad man, just a bit pompous and obviously used to the finer things of a more civilized life in London. The man was a fairly typical, if not stereotypical British aristocrat as far as Bennet could tell from what he'd heard in the club's smoking chamber from the gossip of other members; mostly old men and retired soldiers with nothing better to do than talk about the now daily humdrum of their lives, glorious past adventures and their fellow members. And he thought women loved to chatter and gossip. They had nothing on the aged adherents of the *Empire Club*.

Still, Bennet had met a few characters when he joined the esteemed establishment last year after he moved to London's Kensington district. He'd been against joining at first, having visited a couple similar societies around New York City, but his promised, Anne Creighton, decided he needed to establish himself and get out to meet a select group of like-minded, potential friends. She had suggested the *Empire Club* in the heart of London's Westminster area.

"You'll love it, Billy," she said with that charming grin and a twinkle in her eye. "Daddy's a member, as was my grandfather and you need to make some friends in a circle all your own. As much as I enjoy your company when I make my daily calls, I can tell you're positively bored speechless and so antsy, wanting to leave. Unfortunately I need to attend the occasional luncheon and proper tea to maintain a modicum of respectability in my social standing. Frankly, Billy, you're becoming a bit of a nuisance and a source of conversation for the ladies I visit."

William Bennet grumbled under his breath listening to his pledged, one-day wife to be. He loved her and wanted to spend time with her; that's why he picked up roots and moved to England in the first place. She had been so much fun in Manhattan, laughing gaily and enjoying herself in his company, and wanting to go out every night and see everything on her short sabbatical to America. She was smart and educated and loved to share her knowledge and learn new things, to have adventures and Bennet was more than happy to take her on all he could. They went to museums of course, but they also frequented the popular night clubs and the affluent restaurants around the city. He took her to the top of the *Empire State Building* on a clear day. They walked the length of *Central Park*, and laughed uproariously, huddled under an awning during a sudden rain storm, their picnic on the Sheep's Meadow ruined. He took her to *Delmonico's*, the *21 Club* and *Tavern on the Green*; all the city's best restaurants. And he was smitten, that was the only word for it. She was fun and exciting, and it didn't hurt, she was also quite pleasing to the eye.

He was heart-broken then when she reminded him that her vacation was almost over. He had asked her not to go, to stay with him and maybe…perhaps one day become Mrs. William Bennet. If he had been heart-broken before, he was crushed when she outright said "No."

"I do love you, William," and he knew it was bad news when she did not call him Billy, her pet name for him, "but you have to understand. I have duties and obligations in London; a life at home with my family and society itself. I've loved the time we've spent together, and I've loved New York, it's a fabulous city, but I just can't abandon my family and what's expected of me in the future. I may regret it for the rest of my life, but I must decline and return home and to my lifestyle there. I have obligations. You can understand that, can't you?"

And he did. He on the other hand, didn't have such commitments. Sure, he had a job at his father's company in New York, and he loved the city and the life he led and it didn't hurt that he was wealthy so he could enjoy all Manhattan had to offer. But, with a little finagling on his part, he really had nothing to keep him there. He could sell his Chelsea apartments and get a job in London with the company, as his father's business seemed to have offices everywhere. Surely there was a place for him in that scheme of things in England, and Anne was definitely worth it. So, it really didn't take any thought at all as they shared a fine dinner and danced the night away at the *Stork Club* not long before she was destined to depart.

"I understand," he nodded crushing out his cigarette at the end of the meal, "but, I don't think I can miss you as much as I will after you're gone and still be happy. I'll be going with you."

She stared at him long and hard and he could tell she was considering his sincerity. Little by little though her face brightened and her eyes shined as she finally smiled. "Bill, do you mean what I think you're saying?"

"I do."

And there it was, the almost final nail in his coffin sealing his fate to one day before too long give up his life as a carefree bachelor and become the husband to a wealthy society maiden in London's elite gentry. It would be a life among the upper classes, with wealthy old matrons dressed in the age-old, outdated fashions of their youth gathering at functions like the opera, the races and symphony simply to show off their riches and denigrate their peers. There would be afternoon calls with tea—an endless river of tea—where he would sit and politely nod and smile at Anne's side. Stuffy old men would retire to trophy rooms in their mansions trying to impress with mounted heads of slain animals lining the walls, smoking expensive cigars and swirling warmed brandy in snifters. It would be a life of leisure amongst England's upper crust, with servants and extravagance without a care in the world.

And *god*, how he hated it…

This, he supposed, was why he was here on an expedition heading into the heart of deepest, darkest Africa. Pre-marital jitters, or was he simply trying to hang on to the last vestige of his life as a confirmed bachelor? The wedding date with Anne was swiftly approaching, less than a year now; next June when they would tie the knot and he would commit to her and her world. Even before that though, once the New Year turned, his life would fall into the rut of society's demands and proper decorum and protocol. It seemed every day of that final six months was scheduled with some type of function; an affair to attend and show the gentry just how happy the intended couple were, a new relative to meet and please, another luncheon or tea trying to stay awake.

William Bennet shook his head with a sigh and set his empty tin bowl aside, full enough with stew in his belly he decided. He pulled a crumpled cigarette pack from his shirt pocket and shook one out, lighting it with his Zippo lighter relishing the cool, minty sensation as he took a deep breath. A simple pleasure to be sure, but there were few to be had here in the jungle. He was glad to be here though, despite the harsh conditions and enjoying the company, more or less as he relaxed, glancing about the small encampment the porters had set up. They were relaxing as well; a dozen stout and sturdy dark men they hired in Banana willing to trudge and carry their supplies through the thick, hot flora of Africa's interior for a pittance, men just trying to survive. They were all fed with most already in their bedding for the night, exhausted from the day's march. Those still awake were gathered about their own, smaller fire rolling dice and drinking some homemade hooch they favored; a nasty, bitter concoction that carried quite a kick for those not used to it.

Their leader and the expedition's guide sat with them, laughing hard at some joke one of them told in his native tongue; Swahili, he thought. They had hired Abidemi 'Abi' Abara for his linguistic skills, partially. The forty-ish man seemed to have a knack for languages and he proclaimed to know many of the tribal tongues the company might need on their journey. He was also a fixture in the city of Banana; apparently tops in his field with a wide knowledge of the region and well-known among the merchants and proprietors in that city they would have to barter with. His haggling was topnotch and his men respected him and on top of all that, he was a likable cuss, bursting with tales of horror and excitement to tell about the night's fire. And best of all, Roger knew him.

Bennet regarded Roger Martin for a long moment. He didn't know much about the man besides what he learned in the *Empire Club's* gossip room. He was just a bit older than Bennet, and a Yank Ex-Patriot like himself, though Martin had lived in the Chicago area most of his life. He moved to the United Kingdom a few years before Bennet, why he did not know, settling in Cardiff, Wales rather than London proper. Regardless, he was a member in good standing at the gentleman's club, always seeming to be in house when Bennet visited, taking the Great Western Railway from that southern capitol. Like Saunders, he seemed a good man but far more easy-going. Not handsome by any stretch of the imagination, he was still quite congenial and a well-spring of knowledge. Bennet took an immediate liking to the character for that alone, but too; it was nice to just talk with another American on occasion.

Martin caught Bennet's gaze and smirked, giving a tiny shrug in Saunders' direction. Their portly comrade, despite his grousing, was filling his stew bowl for the third time. Bennet had to chuckle as Martin stepped around the wide fire pit to take a seat beside him on his log of choice for the nightly meal. Settling, the man pulled a silver flask from the pocket of his jacket, unscrewed the cap and offered it to Bennet.

"Trade you," the man suggested motioning at Bennet's cigarette. He smiled and retrieved another from his pack before accepting the gift. He winced taking a swig as Martin sparked a match to life.

"Oh, that's the real thing," he managed to choke out about coughs. His throat was burning as he handed the bottle back. Martin laughed.

"That's twenty-year-old Scotch, M'boy. Cost me a pretty penny, but well worth it I think." Bennet nodded, swallowing as Martin took a long, healthy drink before handing the silver tin back again. He took a long draw on the cigarette. "Figured we could use something special tonight. According to Abi, we should reach the cave by tomorrow afternoon. I figured though, if this whole thing turns out to be a bust, we wouldn't want to celebrate. Better we do so tonight, for tomorrow we may die, eh?"

Bennet shivered a bit at that, but blamed it on the Scotch. Certainly not the best phrase to quote, considering where they were going.

Martin took another long swig and considered Saunders a moment before shaking his head. He offered it to Bennet once more, but he declined so the other man screwed the cap back on the bottle and slipped it back into his coat. "That's enough for tonight, I think; give us a good night's sleep and save the rest for the return trip. We'll need it."

Bennet agreed lighting another cigarette, shaking his rumpled pack for a quick count. He had bought more packs before leaving London, but he needed to pace himself. There was still the return journey to consider. He exhaled looking up into the jungle's tight canopy wistfully, dark and foreboding above him.

"I'm sure you've heard the tales surrounding *Kantor*," he continued after a moment. Bennet had heard many stories concerning the mythical 'Lost City of Gold'. Like Shangri-La, Skartaris, Pellucidar and so many others, it was said to be bursting with riches for those bold enough to seek it out. Unfortunately, all those tales came with the obligatory fables of the dangers awaiting those courageous enough to brave its borders. Martin nodded warming his hands at the fire. Hot and humid as it usually was in the lands straddling the equator it still tended to cool off at night when the sun disappeared over the western horizon. The man seemed well-adapted to the heat during the day. Barely working up a sweat, but at nights he was usually chilled to the bone.

"I've heard," Martin acknowledged with a chuckle, "of course I have. Why do you think I sponsored this whole expedition?" Bennet smirked.

"Right," Bennet took a drag from his cigarette. "What I meant though was the strange tales surrounding the legends, y'know, the alleged, fatal curses and beautiful, exotic priestesses, bloodthirsty headhunters and monstrous guardians." Martin snorted.

"You mean the great, fanged white apes that roam about the caverns and lands leading to the lost city of riches?" Martin laughed out loud, long and hard. "They're fairy tales, m'friend; stories made up to scare away the rubes and relic hunters and keep the children in line. There's no such thing as curses and white gorillas." Martin laughed again, flicking his spent cigarette butt into the fire and Bennet had to chuckle as well. It did sound pretty outlandish.

"You are speaking of the old legends, Bwanas, eh?"

Both men looked up as their guide, Abidemi Abara walked up to join them at the main fire. He was tall and strong just to look at him, Bennet thought, maybe a bit stout from an apparently good life with almost jet black skin and a wide, toothy grin. He took a seat inviting himself into the conversation, sitting on a handy log and taking a long draw of a fat, blunt cigarette like the porters smoked. It smelled of strange, sweet tobacco; not unlike the odors of the old Opium Dens Bennet sometimes visited in London's East End.

"You should not make the fun of the tales, my friends," he continued, his dark eyes sparkling with the fire light, "they are quite real."

"Oh, c'mon now, Abi," Martin scoffed, "surely they're just stories designed to frighten babies at night and to keep away the tourists. Growing up in Brooklyn, I just can't believe in all that mumbo-jumbo. It's a lot of hooey." Abi grinned and shook his head.

"No, Bwana, it's all true. I have seen the *Nyani Mweupe* with my own eyes when I was a child. The great white apes are fierce warriors; savage beasts with much brains. And if they live, the rest must be more than tales too, eh?" Martin stood, laughing as he looked about the encampment. Bennet saw most everyone was already bedded down for the night, including Saunders; already snoring with a belly full of warm stew, a half-eaten bowl at his side.

"Well, if you say so," Martin snorted, "I'll give you the benefit of the doubt, my friend. But that's for tomorrow," he added stretching with a yawn, "it's bed for me now, and I suggest you both do the same."

The two remaining men said their good nights, watching silently as Martin moved to the far side of the fire and crawled into his bed roll, asleep in seconds thanks to the Scotch. Sure the others were asleep or too far away to hear, their guide turned to face Bennet, his visage now grim.

"Don't scoff at the ancient legends, Mr. Bennet," Abi said, his tone and body language altered, his very accent now sounding British rather than African. Bennet listened, intrigued by the change.

"You're not like your friends, sir. I can see that; more savvy and cautious I think. You will listen. They may be exaggerated with the retelling, but the tales of old are based on fact. The city exists, but there are dangers along the way. We haven't seen any of those yet, but we very well may tomorrow, once we enter the labyrinth of the caverns; *if* we enter the caverns.

"There are no *head hunters*, but there is a tribe of fierce and skilled warriors called the *Tonga* who guard the few entrances to the caves. We will encounter them at some point, so be on guard. There are curses as well. I know of no one who has actually seen the city and still lives." He shrugged. "And recall the *Curse of the Pharaohs* of ancient Egypt and the *Ire of Thoth*; *"Cursed be those who disturb the rest of a Pharaoh. They that shall break the seal of this tomb shall meet death by a disease that no doctor can diagnose."* Curse or not, I believe. And I believe in the Priestess as well.

"Believe the legends, Mr. Bennet. You'll live longer."

With that the dark man stood and made his way to his own sleeping area, bedding down for the night. Bennet watched; the camp now silent but for the sounds of snoring men and the crackle of the dying fires.

William Bennet tossed his long-spent cigarette butt into the flames as he considered the words of the obviously well-educated man. He was surprised at the Black, more than he seemed by far, and oddly Bennet felt glad at the man's hidden, mysterious ways. He thought about all he learned long into the night until sleep finally claimed him as well.

And somewhere in the darkness beyond the glow of the dwindling fires, a great cat growled…

The girl smiled slightly as the last of the outsiders finally laid down and drifted off into a fitful slumber. She watched a while longer just to be certain, making sure all the men in the camp were fully asleep as she crouched on the stout limb in the trees high above, hidden by the jungle's thick canopy. After a time and satisfied at last she stood, stretching slightly after her long vigil and began moving quietly back along the wide branch. Once reaching the trunk of the tree she started her long descent back to the jungle's floor, climbing down on the branches and swinging lithely from limb to limb until finally dropping almost silently to the ground a few feet below. Looking up briefly, she smiled.

"Kala, come," she whispered, her hands flicking, beckoning.

She stepped into the foliage, back and away, out of direct sight of the camp, watching above as the deepest shadows seemed to shift and separate. The darkness appeared to take solid form and shape, moving gracefully amidst the sturdier upper branches before swiftly flowing downwards along the trunk. The dark form then dropped and the girl heard the slightest rustle of leaves, the snapping of twigs before the great cat stepped deftly from the underbrush to sit at her feet, casually licking his fur. The girl laughed briefly, biting her lower lip and draping her arm about the panther's shoulders to hug. She put her head to his and heard the low purr of approval rumbling in his throat.

"Shhh, my friend," she cautioned hugging him tightly then scratching behind his ears, "quietly. We must not wake the outsiders. You know that." The mighty jungle cat rumbled again but finally purred, enjoying the attention as the girl giggled.

Jena smiled giving her old friend a final squeeze then standing. The panther seemed content, still muscular and sleek after all these years, but the girl could see lighter patches of gray mingling with the otherwise fine, ebony sheen of his coat. He was getting old she knew; far older than she was herself, slowing in his years but aging gracefully. Still a proud force to be reckoned with; a mighty hunter and warrior she was honored to name friend.

"We'll hunt shortly, Kala, just be patient with me a bit longer," she assured as she peered about the wide tree trunk once more. The fires had dimmed somewhat and a few of the men shifted in their sleep but she still heard the relaxed sounds of snoring, one of them actually mumbling in his dreams. They weren't so different she supposed, not really. Still, they were outsiders; hunters and intruders in the sacred lands and they bore watching.

That was her duty and honor after all. She was the jungle's protector as her mother was for many years before her. Like her mater, Judy, she was now the *White Goddess*; guardian of the lands of the *Tonga Tribe* with all its varied denizens, mysteries and secrets. Secrets no outlander should ever learn. And so far none had under her guardianship and watchful eye.

It was hard at times though. It seemed more and more of the White men were arriving all the time; sometimes in spurts while in others, droves. All were seeking the same things; glory, fame, wealth. They had all heard tales of the great riches lost to the wilds of the Dark Lands; radiant gold and sparkling gems of vast amount and size, all waiting for a man brave enough to seek them out and claim them for his own. It was foolish, Jena often thought and did not truly understand why the Whites put such value on stone and rock simply because it glittered prettily in the sunshine. Her mother and father had taught her of course, not only her numbers and lore, but their queer language and customs as well. Strange ways indeed, but outside of the sacred lands, none of her concern. Let the outlanders do as they pleased in their own lands, but invade her home and steal the revered icons of the *People* and there would come a reckoning.

Movement deep in the foliage caught Kala's attention. He glanced at her licking his lips, obviously hungry. She listened a moment then nodded and the great beast stirred from her side, flowing into the brush and swiftly melding into the dark. Jena gave a final glance at the camp of the outsiders then moved to follow her friend. Smelling the stew had made her hungry as well.

It was time to hunt.

"Bloody hell; why's it so bleedin' hot?" Saunders groused as he crawled along through the tight, rocky tunnel. Bennet could hear the man wheezing with the effort and the heat as his portly associate paused to wipe sweat from his cherry-red face with a dirty handkerchief. It was hot in the confines of the cave he had to agree, but Saunders' constant complaining just seemed to make it worse.

"We're crawling through a volcanic shaft, George," William Bennet explained trying to urge the man onward. "It might not be fully active, but there's still heat and pressure somewhere deep below us with thermal vents and lava pockets churning with the Earth's internal forces. Sometime, maybe millennia ago, lava ran through the rock carving out this shaft. We're damn lucky Abi knew about this 'secret' path, otherwise we'd be struggling to climb the mountains surrounding this mysterious, hidden valley." George Saunders grumbled as he stuffed his kerchief back into his shirt pocket.

"I know all that," he growled, dragging his bulk further along the path, "I don't need a bloody geology lesson. A man can't even comment on the weather, can he?"

"Comment all you want, George, just stop griping." Bennet was about to say more but stopped when he felt Roger Martin's hand on the back of his legs giving it a slight squeeze.

"It's not much farther, Saunders," Martin hissed, wheezing a bit himself. George Saunders huffed but fell silent with that news, at least for the moment.

"Don't fret over George, William," Martin whispered as he brought up the rear. His voice sounded strained as well however; they all did. "We've been slowly climbing uphill since that last fork in this maze. This shaft should start widening soon, and after that, maybe another half-mile or so and we'll be in the big cavern. It won't be long now."

Bennet silently nodded, shining the beam of his flashlight about the tunnel ahead. It was widening somewhat, though he'd couldn't tell the heat was lessening at all. He crawled on keeping Saunders just ahead, marveling at the strange lichen clinging to the gritty walls. Some form of moss he supposed but it glowed a dull green as it was exposed to their lights helping to illuminate the tunnel. He saw insects as well skittering to the safety of tiny holes all along their path reacting to the sudden flashes of light and the noise they were making. Some appeared quite large and a few glowed too; spiders and mosquitos, long centipedes. He hoped none were poisonous.

"I just hope the porters are still there when we return," he commented after a while. The shaft had widened as Martin predicted, though they were still mostly crawling on their hands and knees, pushing their packs of supplies ahead of them. He could see their guide's *torch* beam—as the Brits called their flashlights—along with Saunders' flickering regularly now as the tunnel leveled and straightened. "I'd hate to have to trudge back to civilization without help if we do find anything."

"They'll be there, waiting at the camp we set up near the cave's entrance," Martin assured. "They've only been paid a pittance of what they were promised, and they're greedy buggers, believe me. Plus they're all skilled at hunting and fishing, Abi told me when we hired them. They know the jungle and how to survive, and the Tonga should leave them alone."

"And I figure they all have a pretty good idea what we're really here for. They're too superstitious to go all the way with us, but with a hint of treasure in their heads, well, they'll wait. I'm more worried about the journey back to Banana if we do find something worthwhile. Gold fever's a nasty thing."

William Bennet nodded in agreement again. He'd seen firsthand the effects greed had on a man, and woman for that matter. Nasty indeed.

"Bwana!" Abidemi 'Abi' Abara's voice echoed back down the tunnel from a short distance ahead. Bennet couldn't see the dark man with Saunders' frame taking up most of the shaft, but he could see the darkness was thinning beyond him. He hoped their long, uncomfortable crawl through the mountain was finally at an end.

"We're through," the guide called out with enthusiasm. "We've reached the cavern."

"Thank God ...awwww..."

Bennet scrambled forward as Saunders toppled headlong and disappeared

*…he could see the darkness was thinning beyond him.*

from view leaving the shaft's far opening empty. The man just seemed to suddenly melt into the ground, though William Bennet suspected what probably happened. Still, Saunders' shout of panic set his heart racing as he shoved his pack in front of him towards the egress and the dull glow now beckoning.

"What's that pompous idiot done now?" Martin grumbled behind Bennet, right on his heels. He could hear the concern in the man's voice though, hoping Saunders wasn't hurt though probably more worried about the expedition than the aristocrat. A broken arm or leg would put a quick end to their trip.

Finally Bennet reached the end of the tunnel, pausing to look around at the edge of the opening and get his bearings again. He saw a huge, rocky cavern ahead with another wide opening draped with hanging vines and leaves on the far side leading out into daylight. In the ruddy light he could see more clusters of the lichen lining the stone; glowing faintly and adding to the illumination all around the large space. Stalagmites grew scattered over the cavern's floor while above, stalactites dripped down appearing jagged and ominous like great fangs prepared to bite. A small stream of clear water gurgled from a crack in one wall, running down the rock and cleaving a path across the ground to disappear through another opening in the other side. He saw pools and piles of bat guano and bird droppings all over along with sticks and dead leaves piled up along the sloping walls. And, right below, he saw Saunders.

By the look of things Saunders placed his hand wrong on a loose stone perhaps and the lip of the opening gave way, crumbling under his weight. The man tumbled down the slight incline leading to the cavern floor to sprawl in a heap of dung. He was dirty from his slide and cursing of course but looking none the worse for wear as Abi tried to help him to his feet, trying not to laugh.

"You okay, George?" Bennet asked and Abi chuckled.

"He's fine," the guide assured with a wide smile, "just a little spill. Be careful yourself; the rock's fine-grained basalt and brittle with age."

"Fine?" Saunders snapped as Abi hefted on his arm, helping him to stand. "I'm covered in dung, and I'm hurt," he held up his scraped hands then looked at his elbow, "I'm bleeding."

Bennet shook his head and sighed; pompous idiot indeed. Still, he supposed he better get down there and help get the man cleaned up with the First Aid Kit. He *was* bleeding, and god knows what disease might be in the guano; didn't want him getting infected.

Bennet easily found a safer path down after a quick scrutiny then picked his way to the cavern floor using the larger stones for support. Martin stayed close behind, shouldering his backpack and following Bennet's path and soon the four men were gathered next to the rippling stream. Bennet pulled his medical kit from his bag.

"Let's get you fixed up, George," he urged, dropping his pack and sitting on a handy stone, opening the kit. Inside he found a slim tube of antibiotic ointment, a small bottle of aspirin, gauze bandage wrap and a roll of white tape. The still grumbling George sat near him even as Abi wet a rag from his own backpack to help cleanse the man's wounds. It didn't take long, a bit of wiping followed by a dab of disinfectant ointment and some gauze bandage and Saunders was almost as good as new; fit to travel though not to hear him tell it as he flexed his arm. The group let him complain as they drank from the stream, filling their canteens and relaxing for the next leg of their journey.

"It won't be long now," Abi explained as he made his way towards the cavern's opening. Bennet watched as the man's silhouette seemed to ripple in and out of the glare until he finally stopped near the mouth. "It's overgrown a bit since my last visit," Abi shrugged then turned back to the group and started heading their way, "things grow fast here, and large. I can find the trail though. No worries, Bwanas."

Bennet stood with a smirk screwing the cap back onto his canteen, amused at the way the guide could shift between an educated British university graduate and a semi-literate, local native. The funny thing was, he and maybe Martin were wise to him. Saunders still appeared to be clueless, but was he really worth the effort? Before he could decide he felt Martin's hand on his shoulder.

"Let's get moving, eh?" the man urged with growing excitement. Bennet could feel it building as well as he shouldered his bag and glanced at Saunders. Despite his overblown, in his mind, injuries, the British Lord was hefting his backpack into place, straining to strap the belt.

"I'm ready," Saunders huffed finally buckling the belt about his rotund waist. He rubbed his elbow worrying at his bandage as he picked his way through the rocks to join them. "A few cuts and scrapes won't slow me down."

"That's good, Bwana," Abi nodded vigorously, his white teeth gleaming with his smile, "because the way will be easier, but it could be more dangerous. Be sure to stay close and don't wander off the path. Keep your weapons at hand. Move quiet."

Bennet checked his firearm was still at his side and saw Martin do the same, the other man drawing his machete as well. Both Martin and Abi had described the large creatures the group might encounter; huge beasts seemingly from some long forgotten past, or maybe myth. Prehistoric beasts, he thought by their description…Dragons. It seemed absurd, but he knew most legends were based in some fact. Better safe than sorry.

Bennet let Saunders move in front of him as Martin followed close behind their guide. Saunders stumbled and groused with every step but eventually they passed through the cavern's wide opening through the hanging vines Abi had cut from their path and into the full sunlight of the world beyond. Bennet paused in the tiny area just outside and took a deep breath of the humid air looking all around.

The jungle loomed all about them with trees growing thick and tall, full of foliage and close-packed right up to the small clearing outside the cavern. He could hear the chatter of animals in the verdant green; monkeys and smaller critters skittering along the ground and tangled branches, through the leaves. There seemed a constant hum and buzz of insects too and he was immediately slapping and rubbing them off his exposed, sweaty skin. He heard the murmuring growl of a great cat in the dim shadows deep in the jungle. The multitude of scents coming off the flora was almost overwhelming; sickly sweet at times to fresh then foul like boiled cabbage. The mountains encircling the valley hovered high in the distance; pale blue and lavender with snow-capped peaks fading in and out of misty clouds drifting lazily far above. Things floated in the misty sky, huge and dark.

"Pterons," Martin offered as he peered at the creatures through his binoculars, "I've seen them before. Flocking scavengers mainly, like crows, living off the kills of larger beasts, gliding on the winds and thermal updrafts. They shouldn't bother us, but don't let the distance fool ya. If the air currents change they'll come swooping in if they think we're easy pickin's."

"They're incredible," Bennet proclaimed as he watched the great beasts soar on the air currents, "monsters straight out of the past, still living and thriving."

"Larger?" Saunders questioned checking the cartridge in his rifle with a fierce clack. Martin nodded.

"Much larger, George; monsters to be sure, fast and furious." Saunders harrumphed, shouldering his rifle.

"I'm sure," he puffed, "still, one of those would make a nice trophy, wouldn't it?"

"Something to parade before the *House*, George?" Bennet asked trying to spy Abi up ahead on the trail he was clearing. "Best we stick to our plan, I think. Let's find that city and get out of here."

"You sound afraid, William," Saunders jibed stepping onto the path past Martin.

"Not afraid, George, just cautious."

"There ya go," Martin laughed pushing on ahead, "cautious is good."

Bennet nodded and followed, bringing up the rear.

BLAM! BLAM—BLAM!

William Bennet held his arm rigid as smoke roiled lazily from his .38 revolver, drifting on the breeze. He stared at the great beast; the serpent he just shot in the head, waiting for it to twitch and hiss and rear up once more to threaten them, but it just lay there with its forked tongue lolling from its bloody mouth and its dark, slitted eyes glaring, accusing.

The giant snake had risen up out of the tall grass at the side of the path, hissing as it lunged at Saunders, quickly entwining about the man's legs with astounding speed for something so large. Saunders screamed and brought his rifle about but he was too panicked to take a clear shot, firing a round into the bush so Bennet drew his sidearm and quickly fired. He had felt panic rising within as well as he shot three rounds into the massive head before the monster finally stopped thrashing and dropped to the ground, no longer threatening his associate. Bennet stared at the beast twitching and trying to draw a breath as Martin placed a calming hand on the gun, pointing it down towards the dirt.

"Nice shooting, William," Martin complimented as Bennet staggered, a bit overwhelmed with the sudden rush of adrenaline. "I think you probably got it with the first bullet though. Still, better safe than sorry, eh?"

"What the bloody hell was that?" Saunders shrieked trying to kick his way out of the monstrous coils encircling his legs. He stumbled well back but kept his rifle trained on the creature just in case.

"Boa," Abi chuckled as he crouched down over the dead snake, prying open its wide mouth with his knife; what was left of it anyway. It was a bloody mess. Bennet's bullets had ripped well into it.

"Old one," he continued, "over thirty feet easy, and fat. Pity it's wasted on us. If we had the time, I'd skin it and clean out the meat; snake makes a good meal and lots of money in serpent skin back in Banana."

"What are you on about? It tried to eat me." Saunders continued backing away from the thing, still pointing his rifle.

"Yes," Abi agreed wiping off his blade on a bandana and sheathing the knife, "and it would have, eventually." Abidemi Abara stood and rinsed the cloth with water from his canteen before re-tying it loosely about his neck. "It was just trying to survive, Bwana. All God's creatures need to eat. And the creatures here in this land no nothing of man. They have no fear. Nasty way to die, though." He tsk-ed and shook his head.

"It's a constrictor, George." Martin smirked already heading up the trail again. "Big enough to squeeze the life out of you and swallow you whole. A nasty death to be sure."

"And these grasslands are full of them, and other things," Abi added, giving the boa another sorrowful look before stepping in line after Martin. "We should get moving though. The gunshots will scare away the smaller animals like thunder, but the bigger ones…" He shrugged.

"They get curious at times. And they're all hungry." Martin and Abi moved on, cutting through the overgrown trail, the event apparently already forgotten. Bennet looked at Saunders, finally breathing normally again, waiting for the man to get moving once more, when he was ready.

"You sure you're okay, George," Bennet asked as he reloaded cartridges into his revolver. His portly friend was sweating bullets as always, but he had lost a bit of the rosiness in his puffy cheeks. Bennet could tell the man was still shaken.

"Fine," Saunders answered shortly, stepping over a last length of the dead snake to head down the trail, following the others. "I'm fine," he huffed shouldering his rifle again and wiping away at his perspiration with a handkerchief as he hurried to catch up. "Let's get moving before anything else happens."

Bennet smiled as he holstered his firearm then adjusted his pack. Saunders would be fine with time and a little distance. He'd soon be grousing again about whatever came to mind. So, with a final deep breath and stepping over the serpent as well, Bennet moved into line bringing up the rear again, though perhaps just a bit more attentive to his surroundings. He just hoped nothing else would pop up, rearing its ugly head.

Jena sighed and shook her head in sorrow as she stood over the body of the great, dead snake, Kala sniffing about just to be sure. It was a waste in one sense; so old and mighty to be slain by the foul gun of the outsider simply for trying to feed and survive. It was not right. It deserved a better death. She knew too though that the body would not truly go to waste, rotting here in the sun. She could hear the scavengers gathering in the tall grass not so far away, anxious to feast on the remains. Kala growled sensing them as well. Hyenas probably, as they roved the grasslands hereabouts; their packs taking down the larger animals of the veldt when they saw advantage or weakness. They had no qualm about feeding off the remains of another animals' kill, either. It was the way of the jungle, the law of the land.

She felt an odd sense of relief too, that the outsiders had survived, though she did not understand why. They were mostly cautious, which was good. All but the fat one, who seemed to usually fumble about, loud, gruff and annoying with every step he took. He would not survive if he were not more careful, she was certain.

The other three however seemed to have some sense of respect for the land. She had seen the dark one before traveling through the jungles, and deemed him a true scout; a survivor. The one called Martin knew the land as well, and the dangers they might face at least by his words. But the fourth; he remained an enigma. The man Bennet did not seem to fit in with the rest somehow. He did not seem to want the riches the others sought, nor even the glory. Was he here simply for the adventure? That did not seem the case either. He was a mystery to her and not unlike her father, 'Pistol' Roberts, in many ways.

She was intrigued.

"Come, my friend," Jena purred at last as she squatted and scratched the panther behind its ears. "We need to move swiftly now and get ahead of these outsiders again; reach the city before they do." The great cat looked up at her as though to question her sanity. She laughed.

"I know, I know." She stood and watched the flitting shadows in the grasses. "Better to let them fumble about and meet their fate, eh? But we must protect the city, my old friend, and our land from intruders. You know that."

The panther muttered its displeasure at that plan with a snort, but eventually stalked off into the foliage none the less. After a final long look at the serpent, Jena followed, hurrying to catch up to her friend.

"That's it then?" Saunders commented as he wiped at his brow again, looking on and sounding unimpressed at the sight before them. The overweight adventurer huffed as he sat on a convenient rock, dropping his backpack beside him and resting his Mauser Special British big game rifle against his leg, close to hand and cocked. He was apparently still prepared for trouble.

Bennet was impressed however as he too wiped at perspiration, raking his fingers through his damp hair and fanning himself with his hat. The group had been following the shoddy, overgrown trail mostly uphill for some time accompanied by Saunders' complaints every step of the way to finally peak and crest the rise of a summit only for the jungle's undergrowth to seemingly thin and part to reveal the landscape ahead of them. And there in the distance, about a mile away they could see the white stone of the lost city of Kantor gleaming in the bright sunlight.

It was a massive, sprawling place, Bennet could easily see, but like Manhattan it seemed to be laid out in a kind of uniform grid. Most of the buildings were not overly tall—perhaps three or four stories at most—rather squat and square by the look and somewhat interconnected. He could make out narrow cross streets, which the jungle had tried to reclaim over the years with brush, small trees and draping vines, but he also recognized wider avenues that seemed mostly free of flora and sparkling white like the larger, blocky buildings. Cobblestones perhaps, or something else? Bennet knew something of the problems in construction; stress on buildings, supply issues, manpower needed. But he also had some idea of the wonders the peoples of the ancient world could create. This lost city was no exception.

Most impressive was the great ziggurat at the center of the city. It was a step-pyramid raised high over the city proper on a wide mound with four distinctive, diminishing levels constructed as a receding, terraced compound with the shining white stone that seemed prevalent about the entire city. It was not like the pyramids of Egypt however, which were capped in a point, but more like those of South America and East Asia constructed by the indigenous natives at the time with a smaller building set prominently atop. Legends often told of some god living in that edifice, though Bennet had little clue as to who these ancient builders might worship. They were thorough though, and artisans in many fields by the look as he saw the gleam and sparkle of gold filigree interlacing some of the stone blocks. Bennet felt his curiosity and excitement building as he sipped from his canteen, wondering what they might find within.

"That's it, Saunders," Roger Martin confirmed as he checked his weathered map, "the lost city of gold; Kantor. Our destination's finally in sight. Happy?" Saunders snorted.

"About bloody time if you ask me," Saunders grumbled checking the chamber of his rifle, making certain it was ready to fire with a loud 'clack'. "I just hope it's worth the trek. I better come out with some of those riches I've heard so much about. You better be right, Martin." Saunders eyed the leader of the expedition skeptically and Martin chuckled.

"Not to worry, George." Martin chuckled as he brought up a pair of binoculars to scan the area ahead more closely. Bennet saw more Pterons here still floating lazily in the warm air over the city; some perched on the ziggurat and taller buildings cleaning themselves in rest. He could only imagine what other monsters had claimed the abandoned city for their home. "I'm quite sure you'll get just what you deserve."

"Harrumph…"

"The trail thins out again up ahead, my friends," Abi announced as he stepped back up the rise and into view. He was smiling widely as he slid his machete back into its scabbard for the time being. "It's easy-going and downhill from here, right up to the city gates, just a little over a mile. A casual hike, but for the heat." He grinned looking at Saunders and the man snorted again.

"I hope so," he groused, wiping dripping sweat from his neck and chins, "I'm tired of all this marching about."

"I'd say we should set up a cold camp here then," Martin suggested, replacing his spy-glasses in their case and setting his pack off to the side. Abi nodded his agreement.

"The sun will be going down fast and soon," he elaborated, dropping his own smaller shoulder bag. "Better we're not caught in the city when it gets dark."

"Why the hell not?" Saunders countered in a loud voice. "We're almost there. We can camp in the city, in one of the buildings." Abi shook his head.

"Not a good idea, Bwana," he explained digging a small, wrapped bundle of jerky from his bag and pulling out a strip, taking a healthy bite. "The buildings offer shelter for us, true, but other things take refuge there as well for the cooler temperatures and cover. Nasty critters make their home in the city; more snakes, poisonous and deadly, rats and other vermin that carry disease, insects and spiders. Larger things with big teeth and claws." He frowned and shook his head again.

"Better to enter the city with a full day's light with us." Martin nodded in agreement and Bennet could see the wisdom in their words.

"It'll be fine, George," Bennet confirmed as he started to unroll his bedding off to the side. They had stopped in a small clearing atop the slight knoll, whether by chance or purpose he could not tell. It was free of the ever-encroaching jungle in a small, somewhat flat radius almost perfect for a makeshift campsite. "We could all use the rest, I think. Better to be fresh and at full strength when we get to the city."

"Fine," Saunders snapped in irritation, "What do I know? We'll do it your way."

"Good, good," Abi laughed, pulling a small mesh bag from his shoulder pack. "I'll go see if I can find us some dinner. There's plenty of fruit, nuts and berries for all, and some good root in the area. We'll eat good tonight and sleep sound. Rest now; I'll be back soon." And without a glance behind, Abidemi Abara disappeared into the trees once again.

"I doubt I'll sleep a wink," Saunders informed the others as he undid a knot in his bedroll. "Bloody heat's going to keep me awake all night and I'm sure the air will be full of insects wanting my blood as soon as the sun goes down."

"You've got your aloe lotion, Saunders," Martin reminded the other man as he pulled his own pouch out of his pack. "Lather up your exposed skin well and you'll sleep like a babe."

"Bah," Saunders grumped but did as suggested, grimacing at the foul smell

*"Nasty critters make their home in the city."*

of the lotion. "The stench of this slop will keep me awake for sure, and I want some meat for dinner, not nuts and berries; cor…"

"Just do it, George," Bennet encouraged his associate, already lathering his own lotion into his skin., "and a good fruit salad will build up your energy for tomorrow. You'll see."

"It's bollocks if you ask me," he grumbled but complied, flopping on his bedding to do as suggested. Bennet grinned and settled back, securing his pack against scavenging night prowlers, waiting for their guide to return with his bounty and already looking forward to the next day and whatever adventures they might face.

Jena shifted on her perch in the huge mango tree not far from the outsiders, well within earshot but far enough off their path not to be seen in the shielding leaves. The branches in the old, tall tree were stout and wide offering a good place to sleep for the night since the intruders had decided to bed down until morning. Good, she thought, as she was fatigued.

She had slipped through the thick brush all along the trail the outsiders were following for the better part of the day, scaring off potential threats and sending the smaller animals scurrying into hiding well before the men could reach them. She did not want her jungle friends harmed. The animals would return in time of course, back to their dens and haunts, but in that time she hoped the men would secure a sound campsite for the night, and again, except for the fat one, they seemed to be doing just that. She had no worries as to their safety, or her own for that matter; at least for the night.

She had eaten already as she awaited the intruders to reach the crest of the rise, hoping the smarter ones of the group would suggest resting before their final leg to enter the city. Kala had provided as always, bringing her the haunch of a small, wild dog caught in the hunt. She cooked it over a small, smokeless fire well away from the men and downwind, searing the gamy meat and eating her fill, slicing it off the spit in strips. Not the best fare, but it would suffice for the night.

Now she rested and waited, piercing a ripe mango with her nails and enjoying the sweet, sticky juices drooling down her fingers. She took a healthy bite relishing the taste as she considered the men once more and the dangers they might face on the morrow.

The dark man was not a concern. He was a regular traveler through the lands and knew the ways of the jungle; the unwritten laws and the lost truths within the green. He knew the paths to safely take and what foods one might eat to best survive, and she had seen him, unbeknownst to the others, replenishing the forest all along their journey. He was not a threat to those she deemed friend, and in truth, he was an ally in many ways, caring and respectful of their home.

He, like the man Martin, did not seem a treasure hunter either. That one remained a mystery, as she was not certain of his goals. She was sure he would take his fair share of bounty no doubt, if they found the hidden treasures of the city, but she felt that was not his true intent. Like the Black, he was respectful of the land and knew its dangers. He was not overly wasteful but he was arrogant in his ways and she could tell he did not truly care about the forest. She heard tales of the White men like him, from her parents and the friendly peoples and tribes; exploring the lands simply to see what was there for the glory and fame. But when those men returned to their civilized homes, others usually came in their wake that raped and scarred the green with their stone and steel, clearing the jungle and blasting the land; constructing their ugly, sprawling cities and expanding their choking civilization.

The fat one, Saunders was like that she was sure. The loud, obnoxious *mzungu* was only there for the riches, though she was certain he would take whatever fame and glory came with those. He would return to his homeland, the far off city of London she suspected, boasting of his grand adventures; the travails he had encountered, the savage beasts he defeated along the way and the grand, ancient city he discovered. He would be rich and famous in his land, but then she knew others would come to prove his words and the grand city of Kantor would soon be just a memory.

As Protector, Jena could not allow that to happen. She did not like to kill, but in order to protect the lands and her home she would. Saunders would bear watching.

Jena took a final bite of her mango, spitting out the seeds and tossing the skin and rand into the jungle so another tree might one day grow and other animals might feed on her waste. The circle of life would continue. She sighed then, content with her belly full as she nestled back against the tree's girth and settled in, sleep encroaching. She thought dreamily of the last man.

Bennet remained the intriguing mystery in her final thoughts. He was not there for the riches or glory, she was certain, and though he seemed to enjoy the thrill, he did not simply seem an adventurer like Martin. Something brought him to her lands though. Some inner desire was driving the handsome man through the jungles; some goal she could not fathom. Whatever his purpose, he was cautious and reverent in his journey, treating the forest with admiration and the esteem it deserved. It would be a pity if he did not survive.

Jena smiled as sleep overtook her and she yawned a final time. Yes, a pity if he died, she thought as she settled back against the thick, mango trunk. She would just have to make certain that did not happen.

"It's granite," Bennet announced running a hand over the remarkably smooth, pale stone of the city's walls, "I think, anyway. I'm no geologist. From a distance, I thought it might be marble; just a trick of the light I imagine."

It hadn't taken the party long to eat that morning and then break camp to begin their trek to Kantor. Up before the sun, Abi had bagged some small game that looked like rabbit to Bennet, but skinned and cleaned as it was when he woke to the scent of roasting meat he wasn't certain. It had been gamey and tough to be sure, but their guide had cooked it thoroughly over a small fire along with some tubers and wild radish, spiced with hot peppers in a watery stew, which was both filling and tasty. Abidemi 'Abi' Abara was apparently a man of many talents.

They washed up a bit as they were all filthy from their travels and starting to smell, then packed up their gear and cleaned up their camp; kicking the small fire cold with dirt and burying their waste off in the foliage. Once done with Abi's nod of approval and Saunders' grousing they started off down the gradual slope towards the city.

The path had been easygoing and remarkably clear of growth, Bennet thought as they approached the beckoning city walls. Abi in the lead was clearing some stray flora from the trail with his long machete, but the route seemed well-used in Bennet's opinion. An animal run maybe as he saw small tracks in the dirt, both hoof and claw. But there were larger prints as well; some huge beasts and the occasional sparse human. The mythical white gorillas? Maybe the larger ones, but the others? He wanted to ask Abi, as he was sure the guide had seen them, but he didn't want to scare Saunders and start him on another tirade. Bennet followed along, biting his tongue and hefting the weight of his revolver hanging at his hip for assurance.

It didn't take long to reach the city gates, an easy, downhill walk as Abi explained, but as they drew closer the gleaming white of the walls faded to a grey; not a strange, mystic stone at all.

"It's mined from the mountains at the far end of the valley," Abi explained as he peered cautiously through the broken city gates, "dragged here somehow for miles and put in place with the toil and sweat of many men. Slaves maybe," he shrugged, "I don't know."

"Surely they're all dead now," Saunders piped up sounding unimpressed, wiping perspiration with his kerchief, "nothing to worry about."

"The builders are long dead, George," Martin elucidated as he scraped at a bit of gold filigree on one of the doors with a frown. "But there's others we may need to worry about."

"Others?" Saunders huffed even as something shattered on the hard stone with a loud crack, whizzing past just inches from where he stood. Bennet saw it was an arrow.

"Cover!" he shouted even as a hail of shafts rained down about them, chopping into the dirt or bouncing off the walls. He felt one thump into his backpack as he surged forward, grabbing Saunders by the arm and dragging the stunned man along with him.

"It's the Tonga," Abi yelled as he dashed through the open gates beckoning the others to follow. Martin was close behind him, drawing his gun and firing blindly into the surrounding jungle growth. "Hurry! They won't enter the city. They fear it, and what waits within."

Bennet didn't hesitate as he charged through the gates, dragging Saunders behind him. George seemed to stumble every step of the way but finally staggered through the opening and Bennet pulled him off to the side, out of the line of fire. He drew his revolver, ignoring Saunders as he fell to the ground with an angry huff, peering around the corner of the stone wall but holding his fire. He saw no one, and soon the storm of raining arrows stopped.

"We're safe," Abidemi 'Abi' Abara proclaimed with a relieved sigh, turning to look about the city with an air of caution. "They won't follow us through the gates. We were lucky we were so close before they chose to attack." "I'll say," Martin agreed holstering his weapon. He took a deep breath. "If they'd attacked us out in the open, further up the trail or in the caverns, I dare say we'd be dead." He glanced at Saunders sitting on the ground, "Some of us anyway. Just to be safe though, let's move further away from the gates. A stray, lucky shot will kill you all the same."

Bennet did, holstering his sidearm again and slipping out of his pack. He pulled the arrow, which would have probably killed him otherwise, out of his bag of supplies, inspecting the rough, metal head. It was crude and he saw a black stain lingering on the shaft.

"Poison," Abi enlightened as he gathered up stray arrows quickly tossing them outside the walls, "and deadly. The Tonga are not the headhunters of legend, but they are vicious and territorial of their land. They'll stay and watch, and wait for us when we leave. They're not done with us yet."

"Well, let's hope they get bored and go home," Saunders complained as he struggled back to his feet. He shouldered his dropped rifle and dabbed at his sweat, looking about the inner city. "Bloody barbarians if you ask me. We should contact the King's Regiment at Banana and have them wiped out when we get back to the real world." The others frowned at Saunders for his statement, and Bennet was about to say just how wrong that would be when Abi cut in.

"A good idea, Bwana," the guide nodded with a smile, "but I fear the Tonga know their land and the army might be hard-pressed to kill them all. Many would die, on both sides." Saunders snorted.

"Whatever," he grumbled, "let's get moving then, and find that treasure." Abidemi 'Abi' Abara looked at the man and finally shrugged, heading for the closest wide avenue leading towards the ziggurat.

"As you wish, Bwana."

"You will leave the intruders alone," Jena commanded in the harsh tongue of the Tonga tribe, "they are under my protection while they are within these lands." Kala paced about her legs growling menacingly at the warriors of the Tonga tribe, come to purge the jungle of the invaders. The dozen dark men she could see stared at her, some hanging their heads in embarrassment while others glared, brandishing their bows and spears in defiance. She stood her ground, proud and strong with her hand resting casually on the hilt of her knife. "They will not be harmed."

One of the men adorned with a sparkling stone necklace stepped forward, his feathered spear held low and pointed at the ground. The leader of the hunting party, she surmised as he strode up to her; far taller and more muscular than the others she noted. She stared up at him, her expression blank, waiting.

"The invaders do not belong," he finally spoke staring down at her. He seemed stern, but she saw him swallow in apprehension. Kala growled softly.

"It is our ancient duty to keep outsiders away. You know that, *Guardian*. They will ravage the land and steal the lore of our ancestors. They must die." His spear came up suddenly but Jena did not flinch as he planted the butt into the dirt.

"They will not die," she countered softly, "not by your hand. If they do; if any harm befalls them at your fault, I will seek vengeance. Your warriors will be crippled and lame, outcast in their shame. You will be dead. This is my word and judgement." The taller man stared daggers at the small woman before him. She could see his muscles tensing, his hand fidgeting on the haft of the spear. It was thus for a long, tense moment, until he finally seemed to relax, almost cowing before her.

"It will be as you say, *Protector*," he proclaimed as he stepped back and away. His free hand flicked, his fingers wiggling to sign and his band of warriors scattered into the underbrush. When they were gone he turned to walk away.

"We will not harm them, by your word, but we will be watching until they leave our lands."

"As is your duty, great warrior."

Jena the Jungle Girl let out a heavy sigh of relief as the leader finally disappeared into the foliage. She had been expecting a fight, but thankfully her mother's lessons taught her well in the ways of the Tonga. They would watch and wait, but they would honor their word.

"It's all right, my friend," she soothed, reaching down and scratching behind the panther's ears as he rumbled once more. "They won't bother you.

"Now, after that, let us go and make sure the outsiders don't foolishly kill themselves, eh?"

Kala, the great black panther roared his approval and trotted off towards the city. Jena smiled and followed close behind.

"Do these bloody stairs ever end?"

William Bennet sighed, shaking his head as he followed his portly ally up the long, stone stairway. Silently he agreed with the other man. At the bottom of the staircase it seemed a long, steep climb, but one they could all easily manage with a little effort and caution. The granite was old and chipped in places but mostly solid and set well into place. But as they started their ascent, the number of steps did seem to increase; growing the higher they went. Every time Bennet paused to regain his energy, looking up, it seemed they always had another level to climb. It reminded him of the long, spiraling staircase in the *Statue of Liberty* when he escorted Anne to the crown's viewing room; steep and monotonous, never-ending. He hoped the trek this time would be more satisfying.

Bennet paused on another landing to take a sip of water. He was sweating and breathing hard as the humidity rose with the heat of the day. Despite the misty veil of clouds perpetually overhead, the disk of the sun beamed hot and bright, glaring down on them. One more rise to go, he thought, though he had thought that before.

"It's some kind of illusion in the construction," Martin explained quietly as he stepped up drinking from his canteen as well. "The architects were mages, legend says, which helped in moving the heavy granite blocks across the valley, but they also laid protection in the stone." He tapped at the gold filigree winding through most of the blocks and steps in intricate patterns.

"These are *Runes* of some sort; warnings for intruders like us and probably. Wards written in an ancient language mostly forgotten, I'm sure, but apparently still potent. If we keep our pace and don't get discouraged, we'll eventually reach the top terrace and the shrine atop this cursed ziggurat," Martin sighed and hooked his canteen to his belt, "but for once, I agree with Saunders. Damn annoying."

Bennet chuckled and replaced his own water bottle as he looked up the length of stairs Saunders was trudging. The portly Lord always seemed almost to the top, but never quite reaching it. Abi on the other hand was standing on the final rise. He stood at the top of the steps with a red bandana in hand, having reached the top terrace and waving away the nesting Pterons in a flurry of action. They squawked and shrieked as they plodded clumsily from the landing, diving off and swooping up and out in the open air. They soared high now overhead, circling and watching their nests protectively, ready to return. Abi waved for the party to continue but remained silent, cautious as he watched the skies.

Finally though, after what seemed like forever, Saunders crested the topmost step and stood on the upper terrace. He was heaving in the oppressive humidity and sweating bullets, wiping his dripping skin and trying to draw a deep breath. Bennet saw the man's eyes light up though as he spied the Pteron nests scattered about the upper rise, and the large eggs warming in the sun. Abi cautioned the man as he moved to the closest nest, greed in his eyes.

"Don't disturb the nests, Bwana," Abi hissed as the Lord reached down to touch one of the spherical eggs and probably take it. Saunders looked up at the guide with annoyance.

"The winged-ones will sweep down and rip us to shreds with their claws, Bwana. Leave their young in peace, for all our sakes." Saunders was about to retort, but Martin cut in.

"He's right, George. Don't touch the eggs. I've seen the Pterons when they're in a frenzy; it's nasty and bloody when they devour prey. Let's just keep going. Our riches await within." Martin gestured at the gleaming, white and gold shrine set atop the pyramid. Saunders grimaced looking lustfully at the eggs a final time before stepping away.

"Fine."

The four adventurers moved toward the building in a tight group, circling the large, blocky structure once, inspecting before returning to the northern face. Like most of the city, the stone's gleaming white faded to light gray on the shadowy sides not in the direct sunlight. The rock was chiseled with gold-laced runes and hieroglyphs; pictures faded somewhat with time and the weather depicting scenes of whatever natives lived in these lands ages ago. Bennet saw images of farming and battle, kings, warriors and peasants going about their lives on the wide walls, and sacrifice, death. There seemed to be only one huge, imposing door.

"I wonder if there's an opening on top," Bennet suggested as he looked up, "there seems to be something up there, on the roof."

"An altar, I'd wager," Martin offered, wiping his brow. "At least that's where I'd put one if I was in charge; a place to sacrifice the virgin for all the people to see." Martin gestured towards the city below, the wide plaza and the streets all leading towards the pyramid. Bennet nodded his agreement. It made sense.

"Well, it'd take a lot of effort to get up there just to find a bloody, big rock," Saunders smirked, "literally. There's probably a stairway or ladder inside the shrine and a trap door. Let's concentrate on this door first," he indicated the huge slabbed doorway before them, "before we go climbing up the bloody walls like monkeys." They all grudgingly agreed.

The portal in question was huge; wider than a man's height and twice as tall. It seemed thick and dense just to look at it; the stone somewhat darker than the rest of the ziggurat and etched with a bizarre sigil depicting a winged serpent surrounded by a blazing sun, threatening. The door's frame was lined with gold leaf runes resembling others they had seen but could not identify or read. The pavement stones at the base seemed loose and worn with wear from traffic over the years.

"Pressure plates," Ari explained as he squatted down to examine them. "They were traps once, but whatever they did, their charge was used long ago; stepped on by unwary explorers like us, who died so close to their prize."

"Where are the bodies," Bennet asked, "the skeletons? There should be some remains then."

"Probably taken off by the Pterons and picked clean, I'd wager, fed to their young. They're like vultures in that; scavengers."

"Yes, yes, fine," Saunders griped brushing past Ari and stepping on the stones, "but how do we get this door open? I don't see us breaking it down any time soon." Saunders swept a hand across the door, lightly caressing the upraised sigil.

"Careful, George," Martin spoke up beside the hefty Lord. "That could be part of the puzzle. The stepping stones may be dead, but it's the runes we have to concentrate on and try to decipher some code."

"A secret password, George," Bennet added scrutinizing the faded, golden script etched into the frame. "We just have to figure out the proper sequence, but it might include that picture on the door. Start touching things willy-nilly and god knows what might happen."

*...the four men set to examining the massive door.*

"Poison darts or arrows," Ari offered, "gas… a deadfall pit," he shrugged. "I've seen many dangerous things in old tombs. Best be cautious, Bwana." The man smiled and Saunders huffed.

"Fine," he groused, "get on with it then."

Three of the four men set to examining the massive door trying to make some sense of the petroglyphs, deciphering the runes in the frame and stone-work, the puzzle of the stairs and pressure plates. They were all connected somehow, Bennet thought; some combination sequenced in the proper order to open the great door. The problem was, there were millions of possible com-binations, and they didn't even know if they had all the needed components. Bennet knew the ancient races of the world used staffs and gemstones in their rituals in conjunction with the celestial heavens quite often; the light of the sun, moon and stars, the seasons and the blood of sacrifice. It seemed an impossible task.

Saunders sat on the uppermost step while the others examined the door wiping at his sweaty skin, still trying to regain his breath in the humidity. Ben-net could hear him grumbling as he dug through his pack, pulling out a bag of *Quanta* and biting off a chunk. Like *Pemmican* and simple American jerky, the mixture of dried meat strips, roasted in oils and spices would revitalize the body and sate hunger. It was an explorer's standard survival ration and it would keep for months without spoiling. He chewed noisily as he glanced back at the door.

"You know, it probably only opens from the inside," Saunders offered around a mouthful, "there's no hinges."

"Thanks, George," Martin sniped back, obviously getting annoyed with their current obstruction. Their guide spoke up.

"He could be right, Bwana," Abi agreed. "There could be an entrance under-ground, deep within the pyramid; tunnels running under the whole city with an opening in any of those buildings." He gestured toward the city below. "It would take weeks to search them all, and the surrounding lands, and we don't really even know what we're looking for."

"I suppose," Bennet sighed feeling exhausted and defeated, "I just can't help thinking we're missing something simple." He looked out over the city and about the ziggurat but nothing had really changed except the shadows. The sun never seemed to move during the day but the shades shifted; growing longer or shorter from dawn to dusk. Another queer magic of this strange land he supposed.

"Well, I'll just check on top then," Martin announced as he set aside his rifle, looking at the stone temple building. "Give me a leg up, Abi."

The guide nodded and cupped his hands to help give the other man a boost up. Martin stepped in and jumped a bit, gripping the top stonework and scrambling up the side to stand on the uppermost part of the ziggurat. He squinted, shielding his eyes against the glare as he looked out over the sprawling city and verdant jungle beyond from his new vantage. Finally he turned back to inspect the top.

"Well," Saunders griped, impatient, "what's up there?"

"Not much," the man called back, "an altar slab like we figured; big sucker carved with runes and sigils on this side. It's angled slightly and there's a trench chiseled down the center, I assume for the blood to run off. There's old, dark stains on top of it and a small drainage hole at the lower end dug into the ziggurat's roof." Martin sounded disgusted by that as he moved about the top of the temple.

"I don't see any obvious trap doors or anything though. No way in I can see." Bennet watched as the man stepped out of his line of sight. "Maybe this altar moves.

"Good Lord!"

RAWWRRRR!

Bennet saw something rise from the far side of the temple building. It was just a shadow at first, a blur, but he soon saw long, silvery-furred arms rise up, whipping around wildly. He could not see Martin, but he could hear the man cursing and yelling over the savage roaring of whatever had come up from the far side of the ziggurat. Bennet stood frozen for a heartbeat as the beast's mighty arms went crashing down.

Martin screamed and a shot rang out.

"Bloody…" Saunders croaked out, "what the hell?"

Bennet saw Abidemi 'Abi' Abara with machete drawn running to the far side of the monument ready to help Martin. That snapped Bennet from his shock. He started charging after their guide, drawing his sidearm and yelling back at Saunders to get his rifle. He didn't know if the English Lord even heard him or understood. He had to help Martin.

"Yahhh!"

A black shadow lunged up onto the top of the temple even as Bennet started to round the first corner. He glanced up hearing another snarling roar as the dark mass bounded overhead and beyond. Another scream then and Martin went flying back and out into space. He seemed to hang in the air for a moment then fell to the steps, hitting hard, bouncing and starting the long, tumbling fall down the stone pyramid. Bennet rounded the final corner and skidded to a halt; frozen in his tracks.

He stood gobsmacked to see something out of a nightmare. There was a giant white gorilla, far larger than any regular he had ever seen in any zoo he ever visited in New York or London. Even hunched and railing he could see it was almost three meters tall and massively powerful; it's chest wide with muscular limbs. It was mostly covered in a thick, silver fur now sheened with blood, a great, yowling maw filled with long fang-like teeth and razor sharp claws stretching from its fingers; the *Nyani Mweupe*. It was in a feral rage, locked in savage combat with the black shape he had seen; a leopard, a black panther.

The sleek, black jungle cat was smaller, but only by a little. Just as muscular it was quicker than the great ape, with its own long claws slashing and its snarling, fang-filled mouth snapping and biting deep into the flailing gorilla. It would rip and tear then bound away as the brute thrashed then just as suddenly spring back, pouncing to slash into its opponent once more. It was fearsome to behold, savage nature in all its glory and William Bennet was speechless.

"Bennet!"

He blinked as something touched his arm, breaking him of his shock. He raised his gun in defense but Abidemi 'Abi' Abara placed a firm hand on his arm pointing the gun away before he could fire in panic. Bennet was surprised at the man's strength, his gaze flashing to the other man's machete still in hand dripping blood.

"Don't shoot," he cautioned with wide eyes flicking to the animal's battle still raging, "help your friend." He gestured down the long flight of stairs towards Roger Martin's unmoving form lying still and battered two platforms below. Bennet stared slack-jawed at his comrade, the blotched and bloodied stonework marking the path, but finally snapped back to motion.

"Right," he said as he hurried down the red-streaked stone, hoping his friend was all right. From a distance it didn't look good; Martin wasn't moving but as he descended the stairs two or three at a time he finally saw the body shift, trying to do so.

"Stay still," he cautioned as he dropped to his knees beside his ally. Martin lay on his back and Bennet saw the man's shirtfront was shredded with four long slashes cutting deep into his chest. He was bleeding so Bennet immediately dropped his handgun and tore off his own shirt as fast as he could; wadding it up and pressing it into the other man's wounds to staunch the blood flow. The shirt was sweaty and well-worn but it was all he had, at least until he could get back to his pack. The man groaned as he applied pressure, what first-aid he knew, but Martin was weak, broken and battered from tumbling down the stairs and his fight was minimal.

"Just rest easy, Martin," he soothed as the man looked up at him in confusion. "I'm here… I've got you." Roger Martin did something like a weak smile and his eyes closed again. Still alive; Bennet felt a pulse. He tried to make his friend as comfortable as he could then scooped up his gun again looking to the temple.

His eyes went wide in wonder once more.

He saw a woman atop the ziggurat now joining in the battle with the rampaging ape. Where she came from he had no idea, but she seemed to be fighting alongside the great panther. She was as sleek and well-toned as the cat, but despite her dusky, tanned skin, she appeared to be White and had a full mane of almost red hair cascading about her shoulders. Dressed only in skimpy leathers and animal skins for protection, she was wielding a huge, dangerous-looking knife like she was born with it in hand.

Every move she made seemed poetry in motion to Bennet, having trouble keeping his eyes off her and the battle as he hurried back up the steps. It was like watching a Prima Ballerina in dance; every swipe and slash of her vicious blade well-choreographed and practiced a million times to perfection. Every move was lithe and swift; marvelous.

She was beautiful…

Jena dipped low and slashed into the sinewy leg of the mighty *Nyani Mweupe*, narrowly dodging beneath the brute's sweeping arm and its ravaging claws. She saw a thin line of red where her blade cut; its tough hide protecting the creature, its whole body an armored weapon. It raged as Kala attacked again, continuing his vicious assault now trying to protect her. The creature's fist smashed into her friend's side sending him flying back and away, but like all the great cats he landed well and on his feet before springing immediately back into the fray; striking again with even more ferocity. Jena stabbed again.

She had been scouting near on the lower platforms when the outsiders were examining the *Sun Temple* atop the ancient *Pharaonic Pyramid*; keeping a watchful eye on the outsiders, amused as they fumbled about but wary of the damage they might do. The temple and the pyramid, the entire region was held sacred by all tribes in the area and as she had seen elsewhere many times, when the White men came they usually left a pillaged and scarred land in their wake. It was her duty and pride as the White Goddess and Protector to prevent that from happening. And with her last breath, she would.

But when she heard the grinding noises of ancient magics; stone rubbing on stone and she watched as the *Dawn Stairs* slid down into the pyramid revealing the true opening, she feared. She knew what that meant. The outsiders had angered the Gods and the *Guardians of the Temple* were coming to protect their own.

She was surprised only one of the *Nyani Mweupe* emerged from the temple's dark depths. Still fierce and huge, she could see he was old however; his once majestic silver fur matted in spots and dulled. His bared skin was weathered and wrinkled, and though fearful to behold, time had slowed his movements. But his eyes were bright with intelligence as once again he roared his challenge and slashed at Kala.

Her friend yowled in pain as the sharp claws dug into his shoulder; leaping away and out of reach even as the Guardian lumbered after. The black man was in the fray again as well though; his long knife biting deep into the creature's unprotected back. The man had hesitated when Jena entered the fight, just watching curiously, but now he joined again. The brute howled and swung back blindly as Kala sprang forward in the brief opening, sinking his own fangs into the Guardian's side. Another shriek as the monster staggered. Jena saw her own chance and lunged.

Her knife held high above as she leaped, screaming her rage and her battle cry; the victory chant of the Tonga, she thrust, driving her blade deep into the chest of the great white gorilla. Blood exploded in her face, on her breasts as she forced the tempered metal of her father's knife into her foe, grinding hard to pierce the warrior's heart.

The *Nyani Mweupe* shrieked its agony as he flung her aside; the blade lost to her grip but buried and wedged in place. The brute erupted in newfound fury; one hand gripping the hilt of the dagger, the other arm sweeping wildly, striking out at everything.

"Kala," she called out trying to urge her friend back as the beast grew in frenzy. It hacked the air blindly as Kala dashed aside, out of reach, the black man backing down the steps. The Guardian moaned, working at the knife and striking out at all it could see. But Jena saw it was weakening; its roars softening with pain, its arms moving slower.

BLAM!

Jena gasped to hear the gunshot. It startled them all for a moment, everyone looking about, Jena's gaze darting down the steps towards the man, Bennet. It wasn't him. She looked about and saw the wide-eyed Black craning his neck trying to see the far side of the ziggurat.

She spun about expecting a second Guardian to be lumbering up the steps but instead saw the final outsider; the portly Englishman. He was cursing, standing on the southern stairs and feverishly trying to free a spent cartridge from his rifle to get off another shot. A mighty roar…

Jena turned back and saw the Guardian atop the temple screaming in pain and rage. Its fur was matted and stained with blood now, her knife still embedded in its chest and his left eye shattered, oozing a torrent of red over his face. The once-magnificent beast was dying but still defiant. It ripped her blade free with a yowl of agony, flinging it aside as it howled in anger, beating its chest. She saw it tense before it leaped at the man, Saunders. He screamed in panic but the creature's strength was ebbing; its drive and desire a weakening flame. It fell short hitting the stairs with a heavy thud, sliding down a few steps before coming to a rest, its body still. The great warrior was dead.

Jena felt a wave of sorrow wash over her at the death of the ancient Guardian. She truly wished she did not have to help kill him; he was only protecting his home, doing what he had to do, what he was born and bred to do, like her. But she also felt some strange need to protect these outsiders and she did not know why. Letting the *Nyani Mweupe* slay the men would have been wrong somehow. It seemed more desire than anything, and that worried her.

"The White Goddess..."

She looked up at the voice and saw the Black standing before her, looking on in reverence. He appeared scrutinizing her, as though he could not really believe she was there. She felt uncomfortable in his regard and started looking about for her knife.

"I've heard the legends since I was a child," he whispered, "but I never dreamed to actually see you. You were magnificent. I'm—I do not have the words."

"Is everyone all right?"

It was the man, Bennet, rushing up with his gun still in hand. He looked at the fallen Guardian, then to the Black, the chubby one moving closer with his rifle, finally to settle his gaze on her. He seemed about to say something then held out her blade, hilt first to her, wiped clean of blood.

"Thank you," Bennet said eyeing Kala sitting close behind her, licking his wounds. She accepted the knife and wiped it a bit more before sheathing it. The Englishman finally reached them with his rifle half-raised, lingering on Kala.

"Put that away, George," Bennet urged, reaching out and lowering the fat man's gun barrel, "she just saved our lives, with the help of her friend, I think." Saunders appeared flabbergasted, sputtering.

"That—that leopard? It's a savage beast and needs to be put down. It's tasted blood."

Bennet saw the woman casually withdraw the blade in her hand again as the great cat hunched; both ready to attack. Saunders licked his lips and started to raise his rifle but Abi was suddenly there, standing between them all.

"Do not pursue this, Mister Saunders," the guide commanded, all pretense gone from his voice. "This is the White Goddess; sworn protector of all these lands and everyone within. If you try to harm her," he motioned to the panther, "or her ally, I will strike you down before your next breath." Saunders' eyes bulged and his face went cherry-red as he sputtered again.

"B—b—but,"

"Let it go, Saunders," Bennet urged pointing down the steps, "go see to Roger and take one of the packs. He's wounded and we need to get him out of here. He needs more help than we can give."

"But the treasure," Saunders protested pointing his gun now towards the opening on the far side of the stairs where the white gorilla must have emerged. "It must be right down there. We're so bloody close."

"There is no treasure," the woman stated bluntly, glaring at the Lord. "Any riches within were removed long ago by the Tonga and taken to a place few know. It is reverent to the People and not for the likes of you. I will not allow you to despoil the temple."

George Saunders III stared at the woman several long heartbeats, looked to his adamant allies then finally grumbled; shouldering his rifle and heading back down the ziggurat towards Martin grabbing a pack along the way. Bennet watched the grousing Lord for a moment then returned his attention to the woman, sheathing her blade once more.

"Who are you," he asked looking her up and down, "you fought bravely, magnificently."

"She is the White Goddess," Abidemi 'Abi' Abara offered again as though that were all that needed to be said. Bennet shook his head.

"No; I mean, what's your name?" The woman smiled slightly.

"My mother named me, Jena."

"Well, you certainly saved us, Jena," Bennet sheepishly admitted. Why was he suddenly feeling like a school-boy? "You and your ally,"

"Kala, my friend."

"Kala," Bennet replied looking to the panther who was eyeing him suspiciously, "yes; Kala. You both saved us all. We're forever in your debt." The woman looked at him a long time before crouching down beside the great cat, wiping at his wounds.

"It is my duty," she offered, hugging the panther, "I protect all within these lands. And I will continue to protect you, if you leave the temple undisturbed and take your friend out. Your ally needs aid and there are those in the group you left outside the city who can staunch his wounds with herbs and plants until you get back to your civilization. I will help guide you out on an easier path than how you first entered. But know; you are not welcome here.

"These lands are sacred, and under my protection. As are you," she looked up expectantly, "if you leave."

"Of course," Bennet said looking to Abi who nodded. "We'll have to see to Martin, probably make a travois to drag him out. We need to rest; go back to our camp and gather our things, but then we'll leave."

"Gather what you need," she petted her friend, scratching him behind his ears causing him to purr. "See to your friend and I will see to mine. When you are ready I will lead you from the city, past the Tonga and back to an exit to your lands beyond, where you will be on your own honor, and I will never see any of you here again."

"Of course," he agreed, watching as the exotic woman stepped away; turning her back and starting down the stairs with a slight flick of her hand. The great cat stared at him a moment longer, considering then followed a few steps behind, limping slightly. Bennet watched until they disappeared into the city below. He started as he felt a hand on his shoulder.

"Come, Mister Bennet," Abidemi 'Abi' Abara urged, "We must help Mister Martin and create a travois and leave to rest before the Goddess returns tomorrow. We must be ready." Bennet nodded still watching after the beautiful, mysterious woman. Abi smiled.

"You'll have some wild tales to tell your beloved when we return, eh?"

William Bennet blushed and looked to his new friend; the smiling, knowing face watching him. Bennet sighed trying to remember the visage of his betrothed, Anne Creighton but seeing nothing but Jena, the Jungle-girl. There was nothing to do but agree.

"I will," he forced a smile, "and thanks, my friend." Abi grinned and started down the steps to gather the packs. Bennet watched him then soon followed, his eyes straying towards where the woman disappeared. She was gone.

But William Bennet knew he would see her again and even after he left these lands for a time, he would be back. He would return to her...

The White Goddess; Jena, the Jungle-girl!

**THE END**

# Jena the Jungle-Girl

## Essay:

I had an urge.

Taking a short break from my usual gritty Pulp stories and Fanfiction, I wanted to write something different. Thinking long and hard I finally came upon an idea. Still wanting to write in the 30's, with its Age of Mystery Men & Women, adventuring and ever-growing wealth of excitement, I decided to try my hand at a Jungle Adventure. But just what to write?

Or rather who. I of course checked the Internet for ideas, and there were plenty. From Adana to Zomba the list seemed endless; there was that thing called 'Copyright' to contend with. Many great characters with rich backgrounds and history, but all held in-check with rights reserved, stating: "Use at your own risk".

Only somewhat stymied and now determined I decided—as usual—to create my own. Leaning towards a female Pulp-adventurer in a jungle setting, as there seemed to be a lack, I chose to write an extension of an existing character with a good background. Choosing a 'Copy-writ' female Jungle Adventurer I created her daughter.

Thus came Jena, the Jungle Girl.

Daughter of a previous Pulp-Adventurer, Jena took up the mantle of her mother in the Belgian Congo defending the lands and secrets; all that dwelled in her home. And after much fact-checking and research, the story swiftly fell into place after that.

If you haven't read the story yet, expect a tale hopefully filled with dangerous situations and excitement as a group of explorers delve deep into the jungles of darkest Africa in search of adventure, riches and glory. Thrill to the exploits in a hidden land of mystery. Prehistoric monsters abound and battles for survival at every turn as our heroine—Jena of the Jungle—strives to keep her lands safe from intruders, all the while trying to keep them safe as well.

If you have read my tale, drop me a line or post a Review. Above all; Enjoy! That's what we're all here for.

Curtis Fernlund
kfernland@gmail.com
04-16-2023

**CURTIS FERNLUND** —was born May 15th, 1962 in Medford, Oregon, just a few miles north of the California border where he grew up with his parents and sister. He was raised there and went to school, worked and played until 1984 when he loaded up a U-Haul with most of his worldly belongings and drove cross country with three of his friends, eventually settling in Brooklyn, New York. A few years later he met his soul mate, Erica, and moved to Manhattan to live with her where they spent eighteen wonderful years together until her passing in 2006.

Arriving in Manhattan, he was hoping to get a career in the comic book industry as an artist, and though he did get some work published on occasion elsewhere he could not break into that field. He turned his focus to writing then, and that in Fan Fiction on the still developing Internet, as he had always been a comic book fan as well as of the older Pulp genre and a role-play gamer. After dozens, if not hundreds of stories posted on the Internet, another life goal was achieved, and he became a published paid author, thanks to Ron Fortier, Airship 27 and Erica, who always had faith in him.

Now over three decades later, older and hopefully wiser he's back living in Eugene, Oregon, doing the best he can and of course, writing.

To read more of his work, go to Airship 27:

*Kiri: Night of the Mist in Mystery Men (& Women) Volume 3*
*Kiri: Flight of the Valkyr in Mystery Men (& Women) Volume 6*
*Kiri: Rise of the Bund in Mystery Men (& Women) Volume 7*
*The Queen of Escapes*

# MANEATER

### By Carson Demmans

In the jungle, death is the norm, not the exception. It is a scientific fact that animals in the wild have shorter life spans than those in captivity. The only way carnivores can eat in the wild is to make kills, shortening the life span of herbivores and omnivores. Carnivores, in turn, kill members of their own species or others over territory or supremacy. All animals, in turn, are subject to harsher environmental conditions in the wild which shortens all of their life spans accordingly.

A scientific fact is one thing, but seeing science carried out in the real world is another thing entirely. At that moment, the reality for Helene was that she was looking at the remains of a human being that in life would have covered about twelve square feet of the ground while laying down but that was now spread over ten times that amount of grass. What made it even more horrific was that there was barely any untainted grass in that area. It was all covered with blood, stomach contents, skin, bone, organs, feces, and hair.

Helene had not led a sheltered life. In her life B.K., or Before Ki-Gor, a term she only used in her thoughts and that her husband was only aware of in the sense he noticed her amused grin whenever she thought it; she had been a world-renowned adventuress who sought thrills all over the world. That life metaphorically, and almost literally, ended when her plane crashed in Africa. She had been saved by Ki-Gor, the man who would eventually become her mate.

Ki-Gor stood beside her, looking at the carnage. His only visible reaction was a slight smile, and that was only because he had noticed Helene's gaping mouth and bulging eyes. The beautiful woman with the golden red hair wearing only strips of leopard skin that barely covered her thrusting breasts and genitals had changed since she arrived in Africa and began living with him. But she was still a woman raised in civilization who came to the wild as an adult. Africa was all that Ki-Gor knew, having lived in the wild regions of the continent since his missionary parents had been killed when he was a young child. White children who saw him for the first time wondered how another white person could live like that. Black children in nearby settlements simply wondered how a native like themselves could have naturally blonde hair, and then went about their business. The jungle lord was as much an ordinary part of their day as was death.

Death in this manner was extremely unusual, however. It had happened silently, in the middle of the night, to a Masai warrior who had left his hut and family to investigate a noise he had heard, His wife and family had gone back to sleep, confident that the mighty warrior would investigate, neutralize the problem if necessary, and return safely. Instead, he was still missing in the morning, and the family had sent for their chief, Tembu George. The chief was seven feet of rugged muscle, and to call him imposing was like referring to an elephant's tusks as buck teeth. Besides his obvious physical prowess, Tembu George was known for his fearlessness and leadership skills. His tribe relied on him to always know what to do in any situation.

It was a bad sign when all he could think of doing when the warrior's remains were found was to ask for help.

Tembu George had sent for his close friend, Ki-Gor. The white man was not an official member of the Masai, but the chief thought of the white man as a brother. The best way to describe Ki-Gor was when the perfectly developed Tembu George first saw him, he found Ki-Gor imposing. The blonde man was not the tallest or even the most muscled man in the continent, but he was still highly impressive in those terms. In ancient Greece, sculptors would have sought him out as a model for their statues of their gods. Ki-Gor had not only lived his whole life in Africa, but he had also lived it by seeking out adventure and danger every chance he had, and there had been many chances. Tembu George looked at the man he called brother with pride.

"I was told a great tragedy occurred, but all I see is a dead Masai," a gruff voice barked. Tembu George looked down at the speaker of the insensitive comment.

Tembu George looked down at N'Geeso, chief of the Pygmies, only in the sense that he was almost twice as tall as the older man. Although he would rather die twice as horribly as his tribesman than admit it, he considered N'Gesso to be as much a brother as he did Ki-Gor.

"Speak with respect, ant!" Tembu George snapped.

"He's only whistling in a graveyard," Helene said. The remark was barely audible as she had her hand over mouth in shock as she had just noticed that the one eye remaining in the partially de-fleshed skull was staring at her. The comment was enough to make her three companions turn away from the carnage, as it was even more puzzling.

"The Masai don't bury their dead," N'Gesso said in confusion. "It would be a waste of good dirt."

"Pygmies don't whistle," Tembu George replied. "It would draw the attention of more dangerous creatures like mice."

"It is one of my wife's designs of language," Ki-Gor said, still not taking his eyes off the killing field.

"Figures of speech," Helene corrected. She knew full well that her husband not only knew the correct term but understood the figure of speech as well. Pretending to not understand her was a tactic he often used to divert her attention from anything from scenes of horror like this one or the fact he had failed to take the garbage out as she had asked. "N'Geeso was trying to lighten the mood slightly and make us all feel better."

Tembu George said nothing further. Tribal custom forbade him from saying it about another man's woman, but he thought of Helene in the same terms as he did Ki-Gor, and relied on her almost as much as he did her husband.

"Cannibals?" Helene finally asked.

"If it was, they weren't hungry," Ki-Gor said flatly. He didn't intend the comment as a joke, only the truth. "The body parts have been rearranged, but they are all present. To cover this much ground not even a drop of blood could have been carried away."

"Enemy warriors?" Helene asked.

"Not unless they rode lions," N'Geeso explained. There was none of the harshness in his voice that he reserved for talking to Tembu George. He would never admit it, but he also considered the white woman to be a close friend, and would never harm her in any way, including rebuking her. "Those are the only tracks present."

"Lion!" Tembu George snapped. "There was only one of them, fool!"

"And only a Masai would stand still and let only one mere lion do this to him!" N'Geeso snapped back. It was a good sign. The two black men were only happy when they were insulting each other, and Helene smiled slightly for the first time since she had arrived at the scene of the carnage.

"A Pygmy would have strangled the beast with is bare hands!" N'Geeso bragged.

"Only if he reached up from the beast's stomach!" Tembu George replied. Ki-Gor sighed as he resumed the role he was used to playing with his two friends: referee.

"What did his wife tell you about why he left the hut?" Ki-Gor queried.

"He heard a voice," Tembu George said. "A white man's voice. It was low and he couldn't make out what it was saying, so he went to investigate."

"There are no boot prints around here," Helene's powers of observation were less than the three men, but they had improved greatly in her association with them. "Did he hide in a tree?"

There was a pause in the conversation as the three men exchanged quick glances. When they could not restrain themselves anymore, they all laughed.

"Only if he has the feet of a monkey!" N'Geeso chortled.

"Those are the only marks in the trees, woman!" Tembu George snorted. "You look, but you do not see!"

"It's true," Ki-Gor admitted shyly.

"Are there any signs of baboons?" Helene retorted. The men looked at each other.

"Possible," N'Geeso admitted. "But what does that have to do with anything?"

"Around here, men and baboons are easily mistaken for each other!" Helene fumed as she stormed off. "I think that every morning when I look at what is lying beside me!"

Helene walked with determination into the Masai village. One thing was the same in Africa as every other place she had been: If she wanted to know the truth about a man, she would have to ask his wife.

Helene had been in Africa for many months, but the Masai still looked at her with curiosity. None of them had thought she would stay as long as she had. They accepted Ki-Gor as he was as much part of the jungle as any plant or animal; you could tell that he belonged there just by looking at him. Her flaming hair and movie star features still made her stand out in the village. Men in the village tried not to stare at her, but rarely succeeded; something their wives reminded them of repeatedly. The women usually accepted her but only begrudgingly. On that day, though, when she walked into the hut of the widow, she was instantly accepted as one of them: a wife who loves, or loved, a man who faced danger every day and who knew this could happen to any of them at any time.

Helene said nothing as she looked at the widow but her expression said volumes. The grieving woman nodded back as an acceptance of the respect Helene was showing her. She looked around the hut, and when someone asked what she was doing, she said she was looking for something she could do to help. The widow's friends appreciated the offer but reassured her that they could look after the grieving woman and her children. Helene left the hut, wincing at the thought that she had just lied, but it had been a slight lie that would hopefully lead to a greater good.

She found the three men where she had left them. N'Geeso and Tembu George were still bickering and Ki-Gor was lost in thought. She paused for a second as she approached the trio. She never grew tired of seeing the magnificence of her husband's physique. He sensed her presence and turned suddenly, catching her staring at him. She looked away and pretended she was looking at something, but when she turned back to him, he was still watching her, smiling. He never grew tired of looking at her either.

"Have you found his knife and spear?" she asked. "They're not in his hut."

Tembu George shook his head, embarrassed. He should have known that one of his warriors would never have left his hut at night unarmed.

"Then it was a man!" Helene said triumphantly. "A lion wouldn't take those things away."

"Impossible," Ki-Gor argued. "There are no signs of one."

"There may not have to be," N'Geeso shuddered. "There are two possibilities, Ki-Gor, and if either one is right, we are in more trouble than we thought. It also means that one of your woman's guesses was not as stupid as it sounded."

Helene smiled. The dwarf's chauvinistic habits used to offend her, but she accepted them now. His suggestion that she may not be stupid was as close as he came to complimenting her.

"Explain," Kip-Gor urged.

"There was a full moon last night," N'Geeso whispered. Tembu George snorted.

"Don't tell me that old legend about men turning into beasts in the full moon!" the chief laughed.

"Werewolf?" Helene asked.

"No wolves around here," N'Geeso corrected. "You should ask 'Where lion?' That would explain why the voice of a man was heard but there are only signs of a lion now."

"And the other explanation?" Ki-Gor was losing his patience with his companions, who would often rather talk than act.

"It is the scarier one, my friends," N'Geeso sighed. "Some of my people swear that they have seen baboons riding lions. A lion would have no need for such carnage, but a baboon would not hesitate to be this cruel. If they have somehow learned to control other animals, we are all dead."

"Impossible," Ki-Gor declared.

"I have heard similar stories," Tembu George admitted. "About the baboons, I mean. It would explain some things. A baboon will steal human belongings, like knives and spears."

"And don't they use sticks as tools?" Helene questioned.

"Some do," Tembu George nodded. "But how do you explain the white man's voice? Have the baboons learned to talk as well?"

"I think it means we're looking at the remains of two men, not one," N'Geeso said. "The lion must have eaten most of the white man before the warrior got here."

"What do you think, Ki-Gor? Ki-Gor?" Helene looked around and realized that he had grown tired of their talking and had gone off on his own.

Ki-Gor was glad to be on his own, following the tracks of the killer lion. He did not care if it was really a man or a baboon's steed. He could follow its trail, and he would rather do that than talk about what it might be. At first, the trail was easy to follow as the animal's paws were covered with blood. When that faded, it still left footprints, at least until it came to a stream. Instead of jumping across it, the tracks simply disappeared. It could mean that the lion had continued walking in the stream, leaving no tracks, but no lion would do that on its own.

He was lost in thought when his three companions, gasping, caught up to him. They had run full speed when they had realized he was gone. They were all in excellent shape, but even at their full speed they would never have caught up with the jungle lord if he had not stopped.

"So what do you think it is?" Helene asked.

"A lion," Ki-Gor replied. "For the time being, that is all that we do know and all that we need to know. Once we have avenged Tembu George's warrior we can worry about why the lion is not acting as a lion should."

"But aren't you curious?" Helene pushed.

"Constantly. I will never understand how the three of you look the way you do while having the brains of old women."

Helene fumed but Tembu George put a giant hand on her shoulder to calm her.

"At least he only got your age wrong," he chuckled. The giant Masai had dropped his head slightly to speak to Helene, and as a result the spear flew through the space where the top of his head been, not where it was. Ki-Gor moved like a panther, flattening his three friends to the ground. Tembu George glanced at the spear, which now stuck out of a tree.

"A Masai spear!" Tembu George pointed it out. "Who threw it?"

"I'll guess it was him," Ki-Gor calmly pointed up into a nearby tree. A male baboon screeched at them. Ki-Gor notched an arrow in his ever-present bow and let an arrow fly. It flew past the screeching baboon.

"I have never seen you miss before!" Helene gasped. A larger baboon fell dead to the ground, clutching something in one of his paws.

"He was the only one who was still armed, so he was the only threat," Ki-Gor explaine calmly while the other three gaped at the Masai knife that the dead baboon still held.

"What about the other baboons?" N'Geeso asked.

"They will flee now that one of them is dead," Ki-Gor predicted.

"I agree with you," N'Geeso unslung his long blowpipe. "But I don't think they do."

The troop of baboons moved towards them like a single giant wave of water. Only, they weren't trying to drown the four adventurers but rip them to shreds. Ki-Gor drew his own knife while simultaneously taking the knife from the dead baboon. He became a whirlwind of flashing steel, his animal victims spewing blood and creating a red mist around the jungle lord that obscured him from the vision of his friends.

N'Geeso knew that Ki-Gor would dispense with the baboons closest to him and took aim at the middle of the advancing troop. Again, and again the dwarf sent poison darts with unerring aim. Baboons dropped instantly when hit.

Tembu George used his long spear and long arms to their full advantage. He stabbed any baboon that came within reach in the heart, creating a circle of safety around him and Helene. He heard the scream of a baboon behind him and glanced back. Helene had retrieved the spear that the first baboon had thrown and was using it with almost as much skill as he was.

Baboons are fierce fighters with deadly fangs, but they aren't foolhardy. They had enough intelligence to organize an attack, but also to organize a retreat. The survivors fled. Ki-Gor had done the most close-fighting and was the only one of them to suffer any injury. He bled from half a dozen bites and scratches on his forearms, chest and shoulders, but showed no sign of pain. He glanced into the nearby jungle and threw his three friends to the ground again. A hail of bullets flew over them.

"Don't tell me those baboons have guns!" Helene voiced aloud.

"It depends on your definition of baboons," Ki-Gor growled softly. "Cease fire!" he yelled loud enough for the shooters to hear.

A perfect caricature of a Great White Hunter emerged into the clearing, wearing a pith helmet, long sleeved shirt and a perfectly groomed moustache that was badly out of place in the sweltering heat and humidity.

"Are you all right?" the hunter called. One of his gunbearers laughed.

"That is Ki-Gor Mr. Deer," the native said. "He's more than all right."

"What did you call me?" Deer inquired.

"Sorry," the native sighed. "I meant to say Bwana, that is Ki-Gor. He has survived a thousand fights worse than that one."

"Ki-Gor?" Deer smiled as he stepped forward, holding out his hand. "The name's Deer. Frank Deer. Perhaps you've heard of me?"

Ki-Gor shook the hunter's head but shook his head in response to the question.

"Frank Deer? The circus owner?" Helene quizzed.

"Animal show," Deer replied in a condescending tone. "I had an animal show, not a circus."

"The one I saw had an elephant wearing clown makeup," Tembu George said. "You usually find clowns at a circus, don't you?"

Deer looked at Helene and Tembu George with disgust but had forgotten that Ki-Gor still had a grip on Deer's hand. The hunter winced with pain as Ki-Gor squeezed with a fraction of his strength. At least now he had the hunter's attention.

"Was there any particular reason you were trying to kill me?" Ki-Gor's tone was as nonchalant as if he had asked Deer out for coffee, but the firm grip assured Deer that the jungle man was all business, and extremely serious.

"I was trying to help!" Deer answered painfully. Ki-Gor shrugged as he released Deer's hand. He and N'Geeso grimaced at each other. Unlike Tembu George, who was born in the U.S.A., and Helene, a world traveler before her plane had crashed in Africa, the jungle lord and the pygmy had never left Africa. They had never seen a circus but had heard of them from animal trappers and other white men. The two friends shared a very low opinion of animals being used for entertainment. N'Geeso had also heard horror stories of pygmies from other tribes having been trapped in the past like animals and displayed in circuses and side shows. He instinctively hated Deer. And Ki-Gor held only a slightly higher opinion of the man.

Ki-Gor released Deer's hand and the hunter sighed in relief.

"It is generally best to see what you are shooting at before you open fire," Ki-Gor suggested in a condescending tone. There was a chorus of chuckles from Deer's native gun bearers and guides. His safari was impressed with how much he was paying them, but nothing else. Deer glared at the native men, but they didn't stop laughing to themselves. If Ki-Gor signaled that a man was to be treated like a fool; that was more than enough authorization for them to do so, even if it was about their employer.

"I have heard of you, Mr. Deer," Helene stepped in between Deer and her husband. Ki-Gor's extreme masculinity was one of the things that had instantly attracted her to him when they had first met, but it also meant his opinion of other men was based on how much or how little they came to matching his level. She didn't necessarily disagree with Ki-Gor's appraisal of Deer, but unlike her husband, she didn't believe that the hunter deserved to be crippled on that basis. "Your circus, I mean animal show, is one of the most successful in the world, isn't it?"

"It was," Deer boasted. "I dissolved it. You see, I am a seventh-generation animal trainer, but all of the animals in my show were the same as me: creatures whose entire family tree consisted of animal acts. At some point I realized that the animals I worked with weren't true animals. They were manmade creations that were totally unnatural. I came to Africa to learn about real animals, you see. As my men can confirm, I really don't know much about nature."

"It takes a real man to admit that," Helene shot a disapproving glance at her three male companions. N'Geeso was unmoved, but Ki-Gor and Tembu George looked slightly sheepish for a second. The native safari picked up on Ki-Gor's cues and reluctantly admitted that at least their employer had some self-awareness; it was self-awareness that he was a buffoon, but it was still more than they had given him credit for.

"So, you're learning about animals by killing them?" N'Geeso said skeptically. "If given a choice, they'd probably prefer putting on makeup."

"I'm here to observe," Deer replied. "As you may have noticed, I'm not much of a shot. I observe at a distance, and occasionally trap animals, observe them up close, and then release them unharmed. We hunt a little bit for our own food, but quite frankly my men must do that for me."

"What sort of animals have you been observing?" Ki-Gor asked.

"Monkeys, chimps, baboons mainly."

"Any lions?"

"One," Deer confessed. "Nasty looking brute. When did we see him, men?"

"Too often," one of the gunbearers said with a shiver. "We think it's hunting us, but Bwana disagrees."

"If he was hunting us, we'd be dead," Deer said blandly. "We've only seen him at a distance, but he does seem to follow us. He seems harmless enough."

"Have you seen signs of any other lions?" Ki-Gor asked the gunbearer directly. The man was proud of his recognition by the great jungle lord.

"Just the one, Ki-Gor," the man replied.

*"So, you're leaning about animals by killing them?"*

"Was it alone?" Helene asked.

"Just the one lion," the native confirmed.

"Was anything else with it? Like a baboon maybe?" Helene added.

"Like a baboon riding the lion maybe?" N'Geeso elaborated.

The natives looked at each other suspiciously, unsure of whether to say anything or not. Deer had no doubt about how to react. He burst out laughing.

"Riding the lion? A baboon? Wearing a little cowboy hat and sitting in a little saddle? That sounds like something from one of my shows, not the jungle!"

"We have seen it," the gunbearer affirmed. "A baboon riding the lion, steering it with its mane. At times, some of us have heard the voice of a man, telling the lion what to do."

"It's the voice of a man, but only the baboon is in sight!" another native added.

"Ridiculous!" Deer exclaimed. "Even with tenth or fifteenth generation trained animals, you couldn't achieve that kind of control! And no matter how much training you gave them, you could not teach a baboon how to talk!"

"What do see over there, Deer?" Ki-Gor snapped, pointing at the nearby jungle.

"Trees, of course," Deer answered confused.

"And what do you men see?" Ki-Gor asked Deer's safari.

"Half a dozen monkeys, a couple of toucans, a jackal waiting to feed on the dead baboons…" the gunbearers said. Deer squinted in disbelief, unable to pick out those details.

"These men have spent their lives in the jungle, Deer. If their senses weren't better than yours after a lifetime spent in the city, they'd be dead a hundred times over by now. If you don't mind, I'll trust their senses over yours."

"But do you believe that nonsense?" Deer asked in disbelief. Ki-Gor ignored the man's reaction.

"I believe they saw what they saw, Deer. I believe that they heard what they heard. I'll worry about explanations after I find this lion and kill it. It killed one of Tembu George's warriors, but it didn't act like a lion when it killed. It shredded the man and spread what was left over a space as big as this clearing. It didn't kill for food like a starving lion will, or out of rage like a lion in pain will. It killed out of pure, irrational insanity."

Everyone in the clearing stared at Ki-Gor. Helene had learned to believe her husband no matter how much her new reality differed from her past life. Tembu George and N'Geeso glanced at each other quickly and then turned away, as they always did when they reluctantly agreed with each other. The native safari looked at each other and shivered. Deer simply stood there, his mouth agape.

"Ki-Gor, I don't pretend to understand your jungle. I'm here because I don't understand it and I want to learn. But what you're saying isn't possible. Animals don't go insane the way that people do. Perhaps it has some disease like rabies that's making it act mad, but you don't believe that a lion can go insane, do you?"

"I'm telling you what's true, Deer. Like I told you before, we'll worry about explanations after we kill the lion, not before. The lion follows you, so I'd like to thank you for your kind invitation for me and my friends to join your expedition."

Deer did not want Ki-Gor, who clearly did not like him, anywhere near him. He glanced at the carnage that was once a troop of baboons and which was now raw meat thanks to Ki-Gor and his friends. He also glanced at the natives who hung on every word the jungle lord said. He didn't like them, but relied on them to survive, and couldn't risk angering them.

"You're welcome," Deer muttered, wishing that he had stuck with putting makeup on elephants.

The natives were thrilled with their new situation. They were still hunted by a lion, but now they were protected by the legendary Ki-Gor, who in their eyes was no more a white man than any of them; the jungle lord was a primal force, an irresistible one that was now on their side. The reputation of Tembu George and N'Geeso was only slightly below that of Ki-Gor, and they would have settled for the protection of any one of them; with all three, they would finally sleep peacefully again.

Their opinion of Helene was less clear. The fact that she was a civilized white woman was undeniable; by definition, she didn't belong in their world. Women were not warriors and did not belong in dangerous situations like they were in. They would have little to do with her and not mention her when they returned to their homes.

At least that's what they convinced themselves was the reason; then one of them would steal a look at her perfect silhouette, which defied any racial barriers and made her desirable anywhere she was in the world; then that man would grit his teeth, and briefly acknowledge privately the real reason he wouldn't tell his wife about her.

Deer resented Ki-Gor's presence. Before the jungle lord came along, the natives barely acknowledged Deer's authority over him. Now, Ki-Gor was clearly in charge, and Deer was a spectator on the safari he was paying for. He tried to go about his own business as much as he could independently, ignoring the jungle lord. He was examining the remains of the baboons when he realized that the jungle lord was not ignoring him in return. The jungle lord had silently entered Deer's tent and was standing behind him and looking over his shoulder. Deer grunted.

"I know I'm of no use to you," Deer said. "Why are you here?"

"You know things I don't Deer," Ki-Gor replied bluntly. "I never denied that."

Deer glanced over his shoulder at the face of Ki-Gor. The blond giant showed no sarcasm or demeaning opinion of him. In the absence of friendship, Deer would gladly accept the presence of tolerance.

"I suppose that's true of every man alive," Deer sighed. "What can I tell you that you don't already know?"

"For starters, what are you doing?" Ki-Gor pointed at the surgical scalpel in Deer's hand.

"I'm not a scientist, but I have a little bit of scientific training," Deer explained. "These are the baboons that attacked you and that had weapons. I'm dissecting them to see if there's anything abnormal about their anatomy, including their brains. I failed. They are perfectly normal. Are you happy now?"

"Not particularly, Deer. I am happy that you looked and quite frankly I believe that is what you saw. Is there anything else that you can tell me?"

"There was a camp that my men refused to get close to. It really wasn't a camp, just a rough shelter made from some fallen trees and animal hides. They said it was haunted, and I don't believe in such things. I went to it alone and found a man, a native. He spoke a little English, but it didn't make any sense. Quite frankly he seemed to be a lunatic, but he made no effort to hurt me. He didn't seem dangerous, but you mentioned the acts of a madman, and he's the only madman I've seen."

"I know of the spot you describe," Ki-Gor nodded thoughtfully. "Sometimes tribes have no choice but to exile one of their own if he goes mad and they can't help him. If they survive at all, they sometimes go to the taboo spot you described. Their tribesmen believe it is haunted, and the source of the madness. Instead, it's just a haven for mad people. I didn't know anyone lived their currently."

"So we'll take the safari there?"

"No," Ki-Gor slapped the hunter on the back. It may have been intended as a sign of fellowship, but the jungle lord's massive strength turned it into an assault which nearly knocked the animal trainer off his feet. Many of his old employees in his travelling show had been big powerful men, but Ki-Gor dwarfed them all in terms of raw power. Deer was leery of Ki-Gor. Unlike his old employees, this wild man would not follow his orders, and there would be painful repercussions if he tried.

"No?"

"No," Ki-Gor repeated. "Your men are scared to go see this madman. You are not, and neither is my group. Therefore, that is all who will go."

"But we will leave two dozen fighting men behind!" Deer gasped. Ki-Gor approved.

"Exactly. If we fail, there will be many fewer deaths this way. Pack lightly, Deer. Your best defense may be to run if there is danger. You will at least survive longer than you would otherwise."

Ki-Gor turned quickly and left Deer's tent. Deer thought the jungle lord was being dismissive, but in reality, he had only wanted to turn and leave before Deer could see the giant grin on his face. He was kidding the hunter, but there was no reason for Deer to know that yet.

Deer stretched in his now empty tent, trying to rid himself of the pain from Ki-Gor's slap. He had heard many stories about the adventures of Ki-Gor and his companions, and he was starting to worry that they were true. They had risked their lives many times against fantastic odds and had always survived due to their incredible jungle skills.

Deer had no such skills, but that wasn't what worried him most. He felt another twinge of pain in his back as he realized that he had no choice but to go if Ki-Gor told him to.

Ki-Gor returned to where his friends had set up to sleep for the night. Tembu George was mocking N'Geeso for the pygmy's reluctance to go the madman's camp.

"Nothing good can come of this," N'Geeso muttered.

"Do you believe in ghosts?" Tembu George teased.

"Of course. But that's not what worries me. At best, we are going to face an unpredictable madman. The second worst possibility is that we will find that he's somehow controlling the killer lion and we will have to fight it. And the third worst option is that we will risk our lives and learn nothing."

"You've fought lions before," Helene reminded him.

"Normal lions who hunt for food, yes. Lions who plan murders and brutally carry them out, never."

The pygmy's companions silently agreed with him. An ordinary lion was dangerous enough, and this lion was anything but ordinary.

A mile away and downwind, the killer lion they talked about rested. He was a massive beast made of lean muscle, teeth and claws. He was hungry to the point of being uncomfortable. Game was plentiful, but he didn't dare eat until his master let him. The lion had grudgingly accepted that he was no longer king of beasts, but he was only in his current predicament because his predecessor hadn't done so. He had watched as his predecessor had been ripped to shreds and eaten by baboons. Compared to that, eating nothing but human flesh as directed by a baboon on his back wasn't that bad of an existence. He put his head down and fell asleep despite his discomfort.

He had seen humans earlier in the day. He would be allowed to eat again soon.

Ki-Gor, Helene, Tembu George, N'Geeso and Deer made their way slowly through the jungle. The four residents of Africa could have been traveling at twice their current speed despite the heavy jungle they were in, but Deer was struggling to keep up as it was.

Ki-Gor looked at the circus man with a combination of confusion and admiration. On the one hand, Deer had ignored his advice and not packed lightly. He had shown up with a huge pack that weighed almost as much as he did. However, he insisted on carrying it himself and refusing help.

"Believe it or not," Deer had grumbled to the massive jungle lord, "I am trying to be like you. Let me at least try to do that, will you?"

Tembu George and Helene held no admiration whatsoever for Deer. They had shared what little they knew about the hunter with each other in guarded whispers. In the industrialized world, Deer had achieved some fame because of his circus. The acts were not spectacular, but it was the only one in the world which featured nothing but animal acts. Deer was not only the ringmaster but the only human who did anything but lead the animals in and out of the ring. Elephants wore clown makeup, baboon walked the high wire, and lions tangoed with each other. Many people went to see it, but only once before they went back to seeing more traditional forms of circus entertainment. He had closed his show while it was still profitable, showing that he at least had more business acumen than they thought. He had made shrewd investments in various scientific endeavors and inventions that gave him a substantial income, and then had left the public eye. The public had never cared enough about him to look for him.

N'Geeso had listened to Helen and Tembu George and had shaken his head, not only at the stories they told but at the two of them gossiping. He was the oldest of the four friends, although he rarely mentioned it as he prided himself on, among a very long list of other things, on his physical conditioning. He didn't want to be thought of anything other than a fit man and not just a fit man for his age.

But also on his list of vanities was his judgement of other people's character, and it was his judgement that Deer had none. He accepted the presence of Helene and Ki-Gor in Africa because neither of them had done it willingly. It had been the will of the gods that Ki-Gor had been born in Africa, the orphaned child of missionaries. Those same gods had forced Helene's plane to crash in Africa and that she be saved by Ki-Gor. White men like Deer who came to Africa as a result of their own decisions only did it because they were after something. It was usually money, but sometimes it was spreading their religion or trying to carve their own little kingdom out of the jungle or trying to escape from the fate the gods had decided for them. But, there was always a reason.

Deer had given a reason, but N'Geeso didn't believe it. Deer's men all thought that Deer was a total buffoon, but total buffoons did not shrewdly make the fortune that Helene and Tembu George said that Deer had. The buffoonery was just another act that the master showman was putting on, and N'Geeso wanted to know why.

Ki-Gor signaled for the others to stop so that he could scout ahead alone. This worried Deer. The three remaining adventurers were fearsome and had no use for him. He had known women like Helene in the outside world, but only ever briefly. They quickly grew disdainful of him despite his wealth, and they abandoned him for more impressive looking specimens. As an animal trainer, he admitted that he used the same strategy in picking out animals for his shows.

Tembu George was exactly the type of man that Deer had often been left for. Naturally tall, handsome and powerful, in Deer's eyes the Masai chief had never had to struggle for success or respect.

N'Geeso was the one most like Deer, and that was why Deer feared him the most. Like N'Geeso, Deer had a long list of things that he secretly prided himself on, and his shrewdness in judging other people's character was high on the list. The pygmy would not be fooled by any pretenses that Deer put on, and his ability to appear to be something other than his true self was the number one item on his secret list.

In minutes, Ki-Gor returned. He had traveled through the trees and above the ground, covering miles almost as fast as a bird could have.

"I have found the sanctuary," Ki-Gor reported.

"Is the madman in it?" Deer asked.

"I counted at least a dozen of them, Deer. You had only seen the one they had wanted you to see. The rest were probably busy discussing how to kill you when you came and went last time. I will warn you that they probably have the plan worked out by now."

"I'm not afraid!" Deer claimed with obvious bravado. Although his three friends wrote it off to Deer's stupidity, Ki-Gor saw that it was driven by sincere self-confidence. Self-confidence was necessary if Deer was to remain in Africa, but intelligence would determine if he would do so alive or dead.

The party of five took hours to arrive where Ki-Gor had quickly discovered and returned from in minutes. The main dwelling was a crude structure built around fallen trees with branches, mud and animal hides acting as walls. There were additional lean-tos nearby and something that may have been intended to be a tent but which no rational mind would have mistaken for one. There were ten men lazing around, each looking off into space; a couple of them carrying on conversations with people who were not there or had never existed. They were all from different tribes, with at least one of them originally coming from a mountainous tribe to the north that was several days' worth of marches away. There was one pygmy, amusing himself by piling rocks one on top of another and then starting over with a new order when they toppled to the ground. Tembu George pointed at him.

"Do you know him N'Geeso?"

"Truthfully, no. I can hear him muttering and it's no language I've ever heard. His tattoos aren't like those of my people. There are other tribes of pygmies, but I've only heard of most of them."

"How did they all get here?"

"I have no idea Tembu George. Ki-Gor?"

"It doesn't matter," the jungle lord shrugged. "They are here now. Once we have solved the murder of Tembu George's tribesmen you can wonder about any irrelevant things you want. Deer, do you see the one you met before?"

"I think so," Deer pointed at the largest dwelling. "He was dressed strangely, not like any of these men at all. There, in the shadows inside that structure. I think that's him."

"Then get closer and check," Ki-Gor commanded. "We will be behind you every step of the way."

"Wouldn't I be safer if I was behind all of you?"

"Of course not. Then you could run at the slightest sign of danger, and once you were separated from us you could die in any one of a thousand horrible ways. If you're in front of us, at most you face one way of dying horribly, and we might stand a chance of avenging your death before we all died horribly."

Deer stood paralyzed for a few seconds before he could answer. "Is there any way to avoid dying horribly in the jungle?"

"Don't come here," N'Geeso said drily.

Deer walked forward hesitantly, but only because he knew he could not afford to antagonize the four adventurers. One of the lunatics raised his head when he heard a twig snap, and his dull expression quickly became one of terror.

"Ki-Gor!" he screamed before he ran into the bush. His scream caught the attention of his companions.

"Demon goddess!" another of the lunatics yelled, pointing at Helene, before he and most of the remaining men fled.

"Ugly man!" another yelled before he and the remaining men fled.

"He meant you!" Tembu George and N'Geeso said in unison.

The clamor drew out a strangely dressed man from inside the crude shelter. He had been standing crouched inside the hut due to his strange headgear. It was a mishmash of broken branches, leaves, vines, bark, animal bones and teeth, mud, and some dark material that Helene hoped was mud but which she knew wasn't. The man looked at Deer and snorted with disgust.

"He remembers you," Ki-Gor whispered. "Get closer."

Deer shuffled forward, a strange sight to see in the jungle. Ki-Gor and his friends managed to restrain their laughter, but King, as Ki-Gor had decided to call the lunatic, felt no need to be polite to the type of people who had shunned him. He burst out laughing and was unable to stop for almost a minute. When he finally stopped because he had run out of air in his lungs, he was smiling. King gestured for Deer to come closer, speaking softly.

"He says he should have known you were one of them," N'Geeso explained. "He speaks something close to my language, but he's obviously not one of my people."

"No, he's too handsome," Tembu George said. The giant Masai chief stepped forward, his hands spread wide in a sign of peace. King shrugged, and the entire group moved closer.

"You scared off my subjects," King said. "But they are returning now."

"We mean your men no harm," N'Geeso told him. King laughed.

"My subjects aren't men!" he laughed as baboons swarmed the clearing.

The horrid primates filled every inch of empty ground in the small clearing. Others hung off trees, and still others hung from the ones hanging on trees, all of them focusing their attention on King. King gestured at the baboons grandly with one hand.

"My subjects," he said proudly. N'Geeso translated into English.

"He can have them!" Ki-Gor grunted. He glanced at the other members of the party. They were all staring in wonder, too amazed to be scared, even Deer. The jungle lord told N'Geeso what to say next.

"Do they do whatever you tell them to do?"

*...as baboons swarmed around them...*

"Of course! But truly, I don't ask much of them other than their company. I am a kind and benevolent king."

"And what do you think of the Masai?"

"As little as possible."

"He's not totally insane or stupid," N'Geeso said in English. "Even if he's not controlling the baboons, something drew them here and is stopping them from killing us."

"A Masai was killed recently. Horribly. Were any of your subjects involved?"

"They understand me and love me. I can't understand their language and I can't see everything they do."

"Would they kill a Masai?"

"Probably. I would if I thought I could get away with it. Wouldn't you, pygmy?"

N'Geeso stood silent.

"Can you understand what he said?" Tembu George prodded.

"Of course," N'Geeso replied. "I just don't know how to answer his question."

Ki-Gor gave N'Geeso further instructions.

"What about lions?"

"No, I wouldn't kill one of those," King swore.

"Is that because they are your subjects too?"

"No. For one thing, there aren't any of them around here. My subjects keep all threats out of my kingdom."

"They let us in."

"You aren't a threat. Raise a hand against me and you'll die as horribly as the last man who dared to. My subjects ripped him to shreds before his blow could even land on me, and he was bigger than you. It took hours to eat all of him."

"Could your subjects make a lion do what they want?"

"Possibly. They are very smart. They bring me and the other men food, they build things."

"They sound almost human."

"No," King corrected. "They are better than that. Humans drove me here to die. The baboons keep me alive. No human ever wanted to do that."

N'Geeso gave the rest of his party a summary of what was said. Deer reached a hand towards a baboon and nearly lost it in one snap of the animal's teeth. Deer moved beside King and easily petted a baboon at King's feet. Deer smiled in triumph.

"Don't celebrate yet Deer," Ki-Gor commented. "Unless you want to live here forever within arm's reach of their king, you will have to leave with the rest of us." Ki-Gor gave N'Geeso one final question to ask.

"What kind of things do they build?"

"Well, my crown for one. They left it for me one morning and since I began wearing it, they have been my loyal subjects."

After this last translation, N'Geeso and the others cautiously moved away from King and left the way they had come.

"He must be behind it!" Helene exclaimed. "He hates people, and the baboons love him. If they sensed that he hates people, they would kill one to please him."

"He hates all people," N'Geeso reasoned aloud. "If they wanted to please him, they would kill many more than they have. Besides, I believe him when he says he didn't know that a Masai had been killed. He sounded sincere, and he would have bragged about it if he had known. He had no reason to lie when he was being protected by his subjects."

"They could have killed us," Tembu George agreed. "Or at least tried to. They had no reason to fear us."

"So why did they run when we approached their camp?" Ki-Gor puzzled. Nobody had an answer for that. The party followed the same path they had taken to King, but this time Deer kept falling behind. The others paid him no attention. If he did not want their protection, that was his business. As they were about to leave the thicker part of the jungle, Ki-Gor stopped them. N'Geeso was the first to realize why, as his sense of smell was almost equal to Ki-Gor's. His people had lived in Africa for thousands of years, but he had begrudgingly admitted that destiny had made Ki-Gor as much a part Africa as he would ever be. Tembu George and Helene had not been born in Africa but were learning more every day. They eventually saw the threat that they could not smell. Deer was oblivious.

"A lion!" Helene whispered. "Straight ahead!"

"No, to the right!" Tembu George hissed.

"Left!" N'Geeso snapped.

"You're all correct," Ki-Gor sighed. "There are three of them, and they aren't alone."

"There are more lions?" Helene queried.

"No, baboons. If you look closely, you will see a baboon rider hunched on each of the crouched lions.

"What do we do?" Deer whispered.

"First, we fight," Ki-gor answered.

"And second?"

"We die, Deer. Or we live. It depends on you. You are the weakest link in our chain. Are you going to save us or doom us?"

To the surprise of everyone but Ki-Gor, Deer bravely stepped forward into the clearing after he had taken out his sidearm. The three lions charged as one.

Deer was sweating, but he held his ground and snapped off three shots with his .45. The heads of the three baboons exploded in rapid succession. The lions slowed their charge, and then stopped. They stared at Deer, who kept his gun raised. They turned and walked off. The rest of Deer's party walked up beside him.

"You can put your gun down now," Ki-Gor said.

"As soon as my arm can, I will," Deer gulped.

"Any man who can shoot like that has no reason to be scared," Helene said with admiration.

"Reflex," Deer replied humbly. "Growing up in the circus, I learned how to do trick shooting like that. I acted without thinking. Is that what the rest of you would have done?"

"No, I would have gone after the lions first," Tembu George grinnned.

"Then perhaps Deer is smarter than the rest of us," Ki-Gor forcefully put Deer's arm down for him. The hunter sheepishly holstered his gun and they carried on to the safari camp. The natives who had been left behind had mixed reactions to the story of what had happened.

"A madman who lives with baboons?"

"Baboons who ride lions?"

"Bwana can shoot?"

These natives wanted to carry on with Deer, especially after hearing the new information, whereas the majority had already abandoned the safari to return to their homes. Tembu George also wanted to return to his people to give them a full report.

"The killer lion is dead. They will want to know."

"True," Ki-gor nodded. "One of the lions matched the tracks from your village. But the threat is now worse than it was before. Before there was only one lion riding baboon. Now we know that there were at least three. Until we know that there aren't any more, your village isn't safe. In fact, nobody in Africa is safe."

Deer wandered back to the privacy of his tent. Helene instinctively drew herself closer to her mate, Ki-Gor. To Ki-Gor's silent amusement, Tembu George and N'Geeso drew closer to each other as well. They really were like a married couple. They bickered constantly, but actually loved each other dearly. The remaining natives were silent, on the one hand grateful to be close to Ki-Gor but wondering if they might be safer far from where they were.

The only human in the vicinity who was smiling stared at the three dead baboons King had shot. The smile was not because the baboons were dead. It was a smile of anticipation of revenge; a revenge so horrible that it would make any sane man wince. It was anticipation of revenge where blood soaked the earth, and all men but one screamed in agony. Flesh would be ripped apart at first so that humans would die, and thereafter the flesh could be eaten. It was a vision of Hell that only a madman could dream of.

But, in its own twisted logical way, it made sense. After all, it was in fact the dream of a madman.

It was the dream of the madman that Ki-Gor had called King. He had followed the trespassers to his kingdom to the scene of the carnage, and now he would follow them into their own kingdoms and make them his own.

There were still things that Helene missed about her old life. At first it was luxuries, like fine dining, plays and movies. When the craving for those was gone, she still missed conveniences like electricity, telephones, radio and newspapers. She no longer ever thought about those. After months in the jungle, such things no longer interested her.

However, she would still kill in exchange for a bathroom with a toilet, running water, a sink, clean towels, toilet paper that was actually made out of paper and not a handy leaf, and heaven beyond heaven, a floor, four walls, ceiling and a door that locked behind her!

At first it had disgusted her that Ki-Gor, Tembu George and N'Geeso had no qualms about relieving themselves in every sense of the word in her direct view. Then, it had puzzled her as they did not do it in front of other women. She eventually realized it was because Ki-Gor never hid anything from her, even if she wished that he had. The other two simply no longer thought of her as a woman. She was their brother in arms and blood, it having mixed when spilt on their many adventures.

That did not mean that she felt comfortable relieving herself in any sense of the word anywhere they could ever see her. As far as they knew, she didn't even have those particular bodily functions.

Whenever the four of them made camp, she always scouted the area for potential hiding spots in the jungle for use when nature called. Deer's camp had several, which was ideal. That way, men never suspected why she kept returning to the same bush or clump of trees. It was dark, so she used one of the spots closer to where she and Ki-Gor slept. Through practice, she had learned to do it four times faster than she ever had before she reached Africa.

That practice had been wasted as pure terror scared all of the waste material out of her body in a split second.

A lion had walked within feet of her hiding spot. Normally it would have sensed her, but it was being steered roughly by the baboon on its back and paid attention only to its master and not its own instincts. As she looked behind her, a second lion passed, again ignoring her to avoid the wrath of its baboon master.

A native of Africa doesn't have to be someone who was born there or who was born black. It is someone who belongs there and is part of the continent and whose natural instincts are controlled by situational awareness to make sure that they survive in any situation no matter how bizarre.

Helene wasn't a native of Africa yet. She screamed. Her three companions, however, were all natives of Africa. An objective observer would have thought that it would have been her mate Ki-Gor or the mighty Tembu George who reacted first. In Africa, objectivity means nothing. It was the pygmy N'Geeso who ran to her aid first, grabbing his blowgun with one hand stretched low even as his feet were already running in the direction of the scream. It took less than a split second for him to reach his full speed, which was still blazing despite being the oldest and smallest man present. His age also meant that he had survived under the harsh conditions of the Dark Continent longer than anyone else in camp. He did not question why a baboon on a lion was charging at him. There was no time. He may have slowed his pace a fraction, but he never even thought about stopping as he slid a poisoned dart into his weapon and blew with all of his might. He had learned the previous day that in order to stop this threat he had to kill the rider, not the mount. He was six feet from the baboon when he had fired a dart at it while he and the lion were running at each other, and the primate was dead by the time he ran by its corpse.

Such a shot from a blowgun would take all the breath out of a man of any size, and N'Gesso was no different. What was different was that the pygmy would not let little things like a complete lack of oxygen slow his pace. Every cell of his body screamed as he reached Helene. The baboon who had startled her was frantically pulling on the mane of its lion while screaming in its ears and gouging its hide with its feet. The lion was a giant one and could take the abuse more than the others. There was something about Helene which triggered a memory in its feline brain. It had encountered Helene before in some way, and the foggy memory was preventing it from attacking her. The lion's eyes grew twice a large as normal with the realization that on Helene was the scent of the blonde giant men called Ki-Gor. The lion twitched involuntarily as the healed scars on his body which had been caused by the jungle lord's arrows during a previously encounter throbbed. The lion had barely survived that meeting and had not been the same since. The baboon would torture the lion if he did not obey, but torture was some time in the future, and lions don't comprehend the future well. What they do understand is the present, and the lion could tell that in the present the scent of the jungle lord was coming closer. It bucked harder than any rodeo bronc ever had and gritted its teeth in agony as the baboon drew blood from long gashes on the lion's body and from the now partially severed ear the baboon had bit. Still the lion allowed itself a slight smile as it watched its cruel master die in mid air with an arrow through its heart before it turned and ran in terror from the rapidly approaching Ki-Gor.

With Helene in slightly less peril than she had been, although still admittedly surrounded by psychotic baboons and blood crazed maneaters, N'Geeso allowed himself to take a breath. His screaming lungs thanked him by relieving his oxygen deprived agony momentarily. It was halfhearted thanks at best, because his lungs knew, as did N'Geeso, that this was the closest thing to peace that they would know for the foreseeable future, and the foreseeable future might not be very long at all.

N'Geeso chanced a look over his left shoulder as he smelled another baboon upon him and smiled as the horrid creature's brain matter splattered on his pygmy face. It wasn't the shower of cerebellum which made him smile, but the sight of the man who had fired the fatal shot that had killed the baboon. Tembu George preferred to use traditional Masai weapons now that he was their king, but the black giant was still a crack shot with the pistol he still always wore. There was light from the full moon, but he hadn't needed it. The sound of Helene in trouble had caused a flood of cortisol in his body in an amount that would have killed an ordinary man, but the giant was no ordinary man. The fight or flight hormone hadn't only given his feet wings but his eyes vision that any owl would envy.

N'Geeso wouldn't admit it under any torture dreamed of by any of the fiends he and his friends had faced down the years, and that was a list that even the Marquis de Sade himself avoided in the pits of Hell, preferring to associate with more normal doomed souls like Atilla the Hun and Jack the Ripper, but he loved Tembu George as much as he could any man. N'Geeso would follow Ki-Gor into any battle there could ever be but Tembu George was the man that N'Geeso would always turn back in the middle of such a battle to save. There was a bond between them that was even stronger than the ones they both had with Ki-Gor.

In part that was because Ki-Gor never needed any man to save him in battle. Ki-Gor was a battle in and of himself, a battle looking for a time and place to happen and blood to spill. This was the time and place, and he didn't have to look far to find any blood. He swung his bow back onto his back with one hand as his other hand swung out to grab another baboon by its throat and smashed its skull against a nearby rock. Like Tembu George, his eyes could see at that second as well as they could at high noon. The lions were still coming, but they were all coming from the same direction and ultimately from the same point of origin. At that point stood a howling madman.

"King!" yelled Ki-Gor. It was only a name he had given the lunatic in his own mind so he could reference him and that he hadn't spoken aloud before, but everyone in earshot, which was a large percentage of the second largest continent, knew who he referred to.

That included King himself, and the madman became lucid thanks to his own flood of cortisol, and wished he hadn't. In that moment of logic, he understood the madness of his actions, and knew that he had just been marked for death.

Ki-Gor reached for his bow and to the untrained observer would have seemed to have simultaneously notched an arrow and fired it. To Helene, who had grown accustomed to the various miracles her mate pulled of on a regular basis, she knew that it was a result of the hours of practice that she had watched him perform in the time they had been together. He seemed to move in slow motion to her, a Greek statue with muscles carved from marble that could somehow move at the speed of light without cracking. She saw the arrow speed through the air, but to her surprise it only knocked King's strange headgear off his head and did not enter one of his eye sockets as she had secretly hoped for.

"N'Geeso!" Ki-Gor roared, his voice rising above the roars of the herd of lions. "Stay with Helene!"

Ki-Gor knew that he didn't need to tell the pygmy that, as his old friend had been glued to the side of the redhead since N'Geeso had rushed to her aid. He had said it so that Helene knew that Ki-Gor's thoughts were with her and he was providing for her safety.

N'Geeso grunted. He resented that anyone thought he needed to protect Helene. He also grunted because unlike Helene he felt no need to keep any of his hopes secret.

"Unlike Ki-Gor to miss an easy shot like that!" he grunted. "With that amount of time to aim and fire, the madman should have an arrow sticking out of each eye by now!"

Ki-Gor threw his bow and quiver of arrows to N'Geeso, who understood his friend's intent. The pygmy had no use for what he considered to be newfangled inventions that would never catch on. He preferred his blowgun. But he knew that Ki-Gor had trained Helene to be an expert archer, so he deftly caught the weapons with one hand and gave them to her. She gladly accepted them and fired off her first shot. It was rushed and merely wounded her baboon target instead of killing it, but it was enough to allow the lion it was riding to buck it off and then eat his cruel master alive.

Lions are not clever animals, but they can learn by example if they are properly motivated. Days of torture proved to be excellent motivation, and every lion that had been relieved of their riders followed the example, devouring every fallen baboon. When they ran out of dead and wounded primates, they began helping their brethren by killing baboons themselves.

The lion revolt began where Helene had wounded her first baboon, but unfortunately for the native members of the safari dozens of lions had already passed by Helene before this had happened. The natives fought valiantly, and with some success, but it was far too limited. The lions had snuck up on them in their sleep before Helene had ever left her bed to relieve herself, and by the time she screamed and woke the men up, the beasts were too close to be defended against. Driven on by their cruel baboon masters, lion after lion slaughtered man after man. A lion will normally kill its prey as quickly as possible as they are large animals, and they try to conserve their energy. That only applies if it is the lion that is making the decision. In this case, the decisions had been made for them by their riders, and the baboons cared nothing for the longevity of their mounts or the men they killed. The baboons knew that there was an endless supply of both.

Mombu was one of the few natives who managed to kill some of his attackers. He was one of the ones sleeping furthest from King and therefore the beginning of the lion invasion. He was not a Masai, but he carried a Masai sword. A shrewd man, he knew a good weapon when he saw it. A shrewd warrior, he kept his own motions to a minimum, using only what effort was necessary to make quick killing slashes. But he made the natural mistake of targeting the hard to kill lions and not their more easily harmed riders.

Luckily for his family, Mombu had also been a shrewd businessman and left them behind a valuable estate that would last them the rest of their lives, which was far longer than his. He killed two lions in less than a minute and was mauled to death by the third lion attacking him in less than ten seconds after that. His blood gushed like a river, saturating the handle of his prized sword to the point where no man would ever dare hold it again. It would lay where it fell from his hand for thousands of years until an archaeologist in the far-flung future discovered it, imagining it had been lost in a great battle without ever coming close to imagining the true horror of how its owner had died.

*King turned and ran.*

Ki-Gor moved through the remaining attacking lions and baboons without touching any of them. He knew that his comrades would kill what they could and that the liberated lions were quickly turning the tide of the ambush. Although he dodged and darted from side to side, his path was essentially a straight line between him and King. Even though his madness had returned, King did not need to be sane to know what would happen when Ki-Gor reached him. Even a madman can look at a baboon being slashed into bloody ribbons and know that the same could be easily done to him, and that unlike the lions, there would be no reluctance on the part of Ki-Gor.

King turned and ran. He ran to the jungle that hid his sanctuary, the haven for lunatics. The men he lived with were even more unstable than he was; most of them were what other civilizations would call serial killers, but they had avoided execution because their own people did not know such a term and had thought they were merely possessed by demons. The possessed were subject to exile, not execution, even though in the jungle exile was usually just a slower firm of execution. The men that King lived with were dangerous beyond belief, each one only holding off on their own murderous desires because they were too busy watching the movements of the surrounding men who were planning to kill themselves.

At that moment, King craved the company of those cold-blooded killers more than anything he had ever wanted in his short, deranged life, as it was far safer to be with them than Ki-Gor.

Tembu George swung his sword in wide arcs, killing baboons when he could and backing off lions when he couldn't. He was staying close enough to Helene and N'Geesa to help them and just far enough that he could claim to the pygmy that he had never seen the older man in battle, so N'Geeso must have been hiding. The Masai chief stole what glances that he could to see how quickly Ki-Gor was catching up to King. Having seen his blond friend leave his bow and arrows behind, and Ki-Gor having not drawn his knife, Tembu George assumed it meant that Ki-Gor was going to beat King to death, solving their problem. It seemed obvious that the madman was somehow behind the baboon/lion attacks, as he was the one man who was not in danger.

"At least," the giant warrior mused as Ki-Gor executed a flying tackle on the fleeing King, "Not from any lion or baboon."

Ki-Gor had knocked King flat onto his face and could have easily killed the man with a single blow to the neck. Instead, to the amazement of those watching, Ki-Gor turned the man over and held him down. In other parts of the world such conduct might be considered more sportsmanlike, but there were no referees to be seen that day.

"Talk!" Ki-Gor commanded. The madman tried to comply to the best of his ability, which wasn't very much. King babbled more than any brook was ever capable of, with syllables from a dozen different languages randomly forming combinations that weren't words in any of them. Ki-Gor's reply was a slap that echoed with such force that all other noise in the vicinity instantly stopped, with even the remaining lions and baboons turning their heads to see what was happening.

"Try again!" Ki-Gor snapped. King's body produced more life saving hormones, and his brain came back closer to reality again.

"I led the lions and the baboons here!" he admitted. "When the pygmy told me of the death of the Masai, I could think of nothing else! I was seeking revenge the same way! Please! Kill me quickly!"

"No," Ki-Gor said flatly.

"Then allow me!" Deer said, firing a shot that barely missed Ki-Gor but which killed King instantly, passing through the madman's mouth and tongue eliminating any chance of the man confessing even in death.

Ki-Gor was a blur as he sprung to his feet and backhanded Deer across the face. Deer was knocked to the ground but managed to hold onto his pistol. He pointed it at Ki-Gor but felt the point of a spear pressing into his neck. He dropped his gun and remained motionless.

"Are you all right Ki-Gor?" Helene asked without moving her spear from Deer's skin.

"Is he all right?" snapped Deer. "I just saved his life and was knocked silly for my efforts and now you're trying to kill me, and you ask if he's all right?"

"If she had wanted to kill you Deer, you'd be dead" Ki-Gor explained. "If I had wanted to kill King, you would have never gotten the chance to. If I had wanted to, I could have easily but an arrow through him. I chose not to, the same way you pretended to be an inept buffoon for your men and a shuffling fool for King when you had no problem walking through the jungle with a heavy pack on and you're actually a crack shot. Why are you really in Africa, Deer?"

Deer paused until he felt the spear tip push slightly harder into his skin.

"Do you know who the smartest people in a circus are? I mean a traditional circus and not the kind I had. It's the clowns! They play the fool but they do it so they can get away with being ridiculous and make people the butts of their jokes! I grew up in a regular circus! I never wanted to be an animal trainer! I wanted to be a clown! When I start up my show in the States again, I'll be a bumbling great white hunter! My men found it hilarious! Didn't you?"

Ki-Gor scratched his head in deep thought. He knew little of such things as show business and circuses. He looked to Helene for guidance.

"Your thoughts Helene?" he asked.

Deer screamed as she pushed the spear tip another fraction of an inch deeper into his skin.

"My thoughts exactly," he sighed. Tembu George and N'Geeso joined them. They were scratched in a dozen places each and bitten in a few more. They left a trail of dripping blood from the former battlefield which had been Deer's camp. They had survived a bizarre battle with crazed lions being tortured by baboons that gladly turned on their masters when they were given a chance. They had seen that no other man would ever believe, let alone see for themselves. They had a story to tell Ki-Gor that would stretch even his imagination, which was vast considering how many strange things he had seen. Instead, they saw something more interesting.

"Are we finally going to kill him?" N'Geeso said gleefully.

"Possibly," Ki-Gor said. "Tembu George, search Deer's pockets I deliberately knocked King's headgear off him with an arrow to see what would happen to it. Imagine my surprise when I saw Deer take something out of it when he was running towards me."

Deer blanched at the comments, and even more when Tembu George's giant hands explored every possible area that could be reached from Deer's pockets, some of which was unnecessary for the search but necessary given how annoyed the Masai chief had become with the hunter. Eventually he pulled out an assortment of electronic components.

"King said that the baboons had made him his head gear as a gift," Ki-Gor said grimly. "Even if they were that advanced, they had no source for the parts. You on the other hand Deer, seem to enjoy travelling with a complete laboratory. I saw electronic components half hidden in your tent when I was talking to you earlier. Plus, you had visited King only days ago and would have known where to leave the headgear so that he'd find it. What exactly have you been experimenting with, Deer?"

Tembu George took the components from Ki-Gor and began experimenting with them. He had grown up in America and had some basic knowledge of electronics. He attached a small battery to the other components by hanging wires, but there was no immediate result. Then there was a sound of movement from the nearby bush, and a baboon stepped out. It had obviously been a survivor of the recent battle and shouldn't have been able to walk. Instead, it stood staring at Tembu George. It was joined by a second, and a third, and then a fourth, all of them dripping blood. They should have been licking their wounds, but instead were fascinated by Tembu George.

"Take a step back, Tembu George," KI-Gor advised. Tembu George did so, and the baboons all took a single step closer to him. He gestured to his right, and the baboons began to move in that direction. When he dropped his hand, they stopped again.

"I take it this was an improvement on your original design, Deer," Ki-Gor said. "Both your men and the people in Tembu George's village said that they heard a white man talking when they saw the baboons riding lions. You and I are the only white men in the vicinity, and they don't consider me to be one. I asked your men, and they thought it sounded like you, but knew it couldn't be because you were nowhere near the baboons. That's where your binoculars came in, didn't they? So you could see the baboons and give them orders?"

"How could he do that from so far away?" N'Geeso asked.

"Radio!" exclaimed Helene. In her excitement she made Deer scream, but a quick check showed her that she hadn't caused any serious damage. In her previous life, such a wound would have worried her. In Africa, she had seen insects that made deeper punctures on people than her spear had done on Deer.

"Do you remember how he examined the baboons we killed when we first met him?" Ki-Gor reminded them. "He wasn't examining the bodies. He was removing the radios that he was using to control them from their corpses."

"But they weren't wearing any!" Helene spoke. "We would have seen them."

"They weren't wearing them," Ki-Gor continued. "When I was in Deer's tent I saw his surgical instruments. He must be putting them under their skin. At first, he used his voice commands, and must have trained his baboons to follow his commands, which included controlling the lions. Tembu George, move again, and everyone carefully watch the reaction of the baboons."

Tembu George did so, and everyone saw the baboons wince slightly as they followed his lead.

"They're being shocked!" Helene realized. "I've seen that reaction on animals when trainers have jolted them with electricity. If they don't do as Tembu George wants, they get punished."

"It's far more complicated than that!" Deer said condescendingly. "I taught them to do certain tasks and control them by implants. Originally, there were tiny radio speakers implanted under their skin, but that was too primitive and easy for people to detect. Then, I gave the man you call King a more advanced version. Did you know that the human body produces electrical impulses? My device picks it up and sends it to the baboons. But it was still too clumsy and big. That's why I had to create that huge headdress for King. It was to hide the components."

Tembu George disassembled the electronic apparatus and threw the components on the Ground. N'Geeso triumphantly smashed them into smithereens with a rock. Deer only laughed in response.

"As far as last words go, Deer, that wasn't very memorable!" N'Geeso smirked. His grimace faded as the baboons returned, this time with reinforcements.

"That device included a protection component that kept them from harming its user," Deer chuckled. "Without it, they'll rip you to shreds at my command!"

Helene dropped her spear and threw Deer on his back, proceeding to clamp both of her hands over his mouth so he couldn't say anything. They could still hear his muffled laughter as the baboons advanced. One of them lunged, tackling Helene off a cackling deer. Ki-Gor slit the creature's throat and it died instantly.

"I'm now demonstrating version three!" Deer laughed triumphantly. "No voice commands! No bulky transmitters like you fools just destroyed. They obey my thoughts no different than when my brain commands my hand what to do. They are part of me and I control their every movement."

N'Geeso was about to aim his blowgun at Deer when the hunter moved with surprising speed, grabbing his fallen pistol and shattering the pygmy's weapon with a single shot.

"I'm about to put on a circus!" Deer sneered. "And you four are the star attractions!"

Ki-Gor ignored the bravado of the crazed hunter and drew his knife. If he was to be shot and die, so be it. He did not grow up in the jungle only to have the mistaken belief that he would live forever. His remaining companions would defeat Deer and live without him.

It was an heroic, noble and short-lived thought before he was knocked unconscious as were his male companions by a flurry of rocks. The baboons that threw them swarmed the area. Helene grabbed her spear and ran the closest one through, only to have the spear pulled from her from the opposite side of the now dead baboon. She was grabbed from behind and her hands bound with her own clothing, which had been roughly ripped from her body by baboons. She shuddered at the memory of what Deer had bragged: the baboons were now only an extension of his own body, and in effect it was hands who stripped and bound her. She looked at Deer with disgust.

"I saw lots of rope in your camp, Deer," she muttered.

She was grabbed by her long hair by two baboons and dragged unceremoniously into the jungle, with the three unconscious males being dragged cruelly by the feet, their head smashing against all rocks in the path towards Deer's secret camp. It was where he had disappeared to when his main safari had thought he had just wandered off by himself. He had hired other natives to build it and help in the initial training of the baboon army, only to become the first victims of the baboon army. They had been ripped to shreds, a sight that had awoken a long-forgotten childhood memory. Deer had seen a circus hand killed in a similar fashion in his father's circus, and his father had summarily had the animals slaughtered in front of the boy. It had been intended to be a lesson in the harsh realities of training wild animals.

Instead, it had subconsciously become the driving force of Deer's life: to one day be able to have the ability to kill like a wild animal, but to be able to escape the punishment the killer baboons had by virtue of being human. Unknown to Deer's father, the baboons had been goaded and released by Deer in order to kill the circus laborer.

Ki-Gor regained consciousness and found himself on the ground, unbound. Helene stood nearby, dressed in a garish showgirl costume. The costume was poorly adjusted on her, and then he deduced by the scratches on her body that she had not dressed herself but had been dressed by the baboons that surrounded the clearing he and his friends were in. The baboons were sitting on crude wooden benches which they didn't need but helped create the illusion that they were the spectators of what Deer had always wanted to achieve: a circus of blood that would for once entertain him and not the useless customers who mocked him and his efforts but which he was forced to endure in order to make a living.

Ki-Gor looked to either side and saw that N'Geeso and Tembu George were nearby, and that each of them was inside a circle of rocks. Ki-Gor didn't understand it at the time, but the rocks were rings, and he was in the center one, the intended star attraction of a nightmare circus.

Helene forced herself to grin as she had been ordered to. She was playing along in the vain hope that a chance of escape would present itself. Deer had told her that he had only kept them alive since he first met them for this very moment, when he could exact revenge on them as an example of the smug bastards who had dared provided him with a living in his previous life.

Deer entered the clearing and the baboons cheered, but as they were under his control it was actually Deer cheering himself. He had painfully managed to implant the necessary circuitry under his own skin without the benefit of anesthesia, but the agony had been worth it. The baboons obeyed his every whim instantly. He was dressed in his father's old ringmaster costume. Personally, he had never worn one in his own circus, but for this performance he wanted to mock the man who had forced him into the circus world he grew to hate, a surrogate execution he had never had the guts to carry out when his father was alive.

Ki-Gor twitched and saw Helene gasp for breath as a baboon yanked on the lariat around her neck. He froze and she could breathe again. He grimaced. If Deer had threatened Ki-Gor's life, the jungle lord would not have flinched. With his mate being threatened, he was powerless.

In unison, three baboons holding torches marched forward, each setting fire to a hoop made from branches in each of the three rings.

"Tell them what to do, Helene," Deer commanded. He wanted her to be the cause of any harm her friends suffered. She had seen similar situations in circuses and knew what came next.

"Jump through the hoops!" she gasped.

N'Geeso surged forward to be the first to risk life and limb. His hoop was mounted on a stick well above his height, but his leg strength was disproportionate to his size. He passed through the hoop unscathed except for his pride, which was the most sensitive part of his anatomy.

Tembu George followed. His hoop was set even higher than the pygmy's, which was not a problem, but its small diameter was. The hoop was made strong enough that it did not break when his sides hit it. It flexed enough to let him through, but only barely, and with burns to his ribs.

Ki-Gor stared at his hoop in disgust it was the highest, strongest and smallest of the three.

"Jump through it or she dies!" Deer said.

"Come closer, king of baboons! I can't hear you over the screams of your subjects!" Ki-Gor yelled. Deer closed the distance between him and the jungle lord, but Ki-Gor acted before the hunter could repeat his words or guess Ki-Gor's true motive.

Ki-Gor ran towards the hoop and leapt, but as he did so he somersaulted in midair so that it was his feet that made first contact with the flaming hoop instead of passing through with his extended arms first as had N'Geeso and Tembu George. Flames provided little discomfort to soles of feet that had spent a lifetime going over rocks, thorns and rough trails. Gripping the hoop with the arches of his feet, his momentum ripped it free of its support. Deer was mesmerized by the incredible arc Ki'Gor's body took. He had seen many acrobats in his childhood in the circus, but none equaled the feats of Ki-Gor.

Ki'Gor completed his midair somersault by jamming the flaming hoop over Deer's head, pinning his arms to his side. Deer's ancient ringmaster suit was dry with age and burst into flame like dry tinder. Like many sadists, Deer had no qualms about inflicting pain on others but had no tolerance for it himself. He screamed louder than he ever had before in his life, and he screamed the only word that filled his mind.

"Water!"

Deer's subjects, as Ki-Gor had referred to the baboons in attendance, obliged. They surged towards Deer as one, including the one who had been holding Helene's deadly leash. The baboons grabbed Deer by his unburning parts and forced his entire body into the nearest source of water, a large barrel filled with rainwater. Dear was in shock and unable to give another mental command, and shortly thereafter his brain was unable to do anything at all ever again. The infernal chattering inside their heads was gone and they could move again without the pain of electric shock, so the baboons peacefully disbursed, some of them casually brushing against Ki-Gor and company in the process.

"Where are my clothes so I can get out of this ridiculous costume?" Helene asked. Her jungle attire was scanty by civilized standards, but the costume Deer had forced her ample figure to be stuffed into was smaller than the dresses worn by a child's doll.

"No idea!" N'Geeso said sweetly as he kicked her animal skin outfit further under a bush.

Ki-Gor went to the rain barrel and pulled Deer out. He had been stuffed in headfirst making his drowning inevitable with his arms bound by the hoop. Still, in the jungle it never hurt to check to see how dead your opponent was. He unceremoniously dumped the corpse in the jungle and did not bother to look back to see what scavengers were already busy dining on it.

"I need clothes!" Helene screeched.

"We all do, but we'll live with what we have," Ki-Gor smiled, once again pretending to not know what she meant. N'Geeso and Tembu George nodded in happy agreement.

**THE END**

# JUNGLE HEROES

**W**ithout Tarzan, there never would have been Ki-Gor, but that is hardly a criticism when you consider that in the opinion of many people, including Rudyard Kipling, that without *The Jungle Book* there would have been no Tarzan. Ki-Gor is arguable closer to Tarzan than Tarzan is to Mowgli, but mainly because they both originated in pulp magazines.

Still, there are many differences between Ki-Gor and Tarzan. Ki-Gor was a product of the Fiction House pulps, and Tarzan first appeared in Munsey titles. Those two publishers may have both been pulps, but only because of the paper they were printed on. Fiction House was far more lurid and less serious in its content.

The lurid details are obvious, but the less serious tone is more subtle, mainly in the bantering between the four main characters. Tarzan was often a solo act, but Ki-Gor was almost always with his three comrades. His wife Helene was no shrinking violet, but also had a shrill side that was closer to Molly of *Fibber McGee and Molly* fame than Tarzan's Jane. N'Geeso and Tembu George were mighty warriors in action, but in conversation were closer to Abbott and Costello than any ERB character.

The Tarzan stories weren't always humorless but were nowhere near the level of comedies that the Ki-Gor stories were, although admittedly I have read more of the former than the latter. The ones I have read were far lighter reading than the average Tarzan novel, however, and I have tried to capture that in my story.

The villain's name is based on Frank Buck, famed author of *Bring 'Em Back Alive,* but his character is based on the countless stock characters in countless jungle stories and movies based on Buck. Look up a picture of him, and then count how many white hunters in pith helmets and moustaches you've encountered in your life.

It will take awhile and be an unpleasant boring chore.

Hopefully reading my story will be quick, easy and fun by comparison.

**CARSON DEMMANS** - is a freelance writer in Regina SK, Canada. Since 1994, he has been published more than 1500 times, with sales varying from a single sentence for cartoon gags to newspaper columns, magazine articles, and short stories. He is the author of four books so far, with more in the works. The first three are regional humor, but his most recent one is OH MY GOD! THEY PRINTED THAT?, a history/satire of sexist and racist comic books. If you like books about pop culture history, check it out on Amazon or at Bear Manor Media. He needs the money.

# The Curse of the Queen

## by Terry Wijesuriya

**"I**'m here to speak to Captain Ryan." It was a statement, not a query. The corporal looked up from the paperwork on his desk and saw a young black man, neatly dressed in European clothing, standing in front of him. He was surprised- not at the sight of a black man in itself, but because the voice that had spoken a moment ago had a clipped British accent.

"Natives round the back," the corporal said, automatically.

The man drew himself up haughtily. "I beg your pardon, but I am not a native."

"You're black, aren't you?" asked the corporal, without rancor but also without courtesy.

"I am from Rhodesia, and therefore I cannot be native to the Congo. The Captain is expecting me," the man stated, frostily.

"What is your business with him?" the corporal asked, a little more politely, looking curiously at the man.

"I have corresponded with him, regarding travelling into the Ituri forest," the man began. "I was told to report to him once I arrived here in Livingstone."

"Please take a seat," the corporal said, rising, "I will ask Captain Ryan."

The man sat down on the hard benches that lined the open verandah. The heat outside was oppressive, and the dust on the road rose up in little hur-

82

ricanes every time a cart went past. Some children scuffled around in the dry grass by the side of the road. The man had just started watching them when the corporal returned.

"Your name, please?"

"Oh," the man started, "Mpumelelo Matthias. Tell Captain Ryan that I am the anthropologist."

The corporal nodded and withdrew.

Mpumelelo Matthias turned back to the scene outside. *So many black people*, he thought, only half-pleased. He thought about his proposed study and he wondered for the hundredth time whether he could do something, whether it could be accepted, or whether people would see his name, Mpumelelo, and disregard his work because he was black.

"Captain Ryan will see you now," the corporal announced.

Mpumelelo got to his feet with alacrity, and headed in to where the corporal held the door open for him.

Inside the office, cooled by one ancient wooden-bladed fan, a burly man with the weathered skin and bleached hair of the European born in the tropics rose and held out a hand.

"Dr. Matthias, I presume," he inquired, with only a trace of amusement in his sober face.

Mpumelelo grinned at him, shaking his hand. Both men sat down.

"You explained your plan to me via letter, but perhaps you could run over the main points again?" Captain Ryan leant back in his chair.

"Yes. I plan to go into the Ituri forest in order to carry out an anthropological study of the BaMbuti people." Mpumelelo paused, and then continued with a little laugh. "That's the main point, but where I'd need your assistance is to actually head into the forest. Theoretically, I know where the BaMbuti can be found, but practically I know that I have a very slim chance of actually finding them unless I had someone like yourself to perhaps introduce me, as it were."

"Hm," said Captain Ryan. "The pygmies are notoriously hard to get hold of if they don't want to talk."

"Your name was recommended to me as a man who got on well with the pygmies," Mpumelelo explained.

Ryan laughed. "I think it's more a case of them finding me amusing and sometimes useful, but I will do what I can. I think the best option would be for me to take you down the river to the closest Negro village. If I have the time, I will take you to the BaMbuti themselves, but if not, I will introduce you to some people who can. How does that sound?"

Mpumelelo nodded eagerly. "It sounds like an excellent plan."

"Will you be taking in much equipment?" Ryan asked.

"Just my notebooks," Mpumelelo answered. "I may return with a camera if this first visit goes well."

Ryan nodded. "We will discuss logistics later. Now, how about something to drink?"

Iced drinks in hand, Ryan led the way to the back verandah, which was overhung by a large tree and so was shadier than the front. Two comfortable cane chairs were placed there, facing the large garden.

"What do you know about the BaMbuti?" Ryan asked, settling down in one chair.

Mpumelelo inclined his head modestly. "As much as anyone could know who hasn't actually lived with them."

Ryan nodded. "You've read Father Schebesta's work?"

Mpumelelo acquiesced guardedly, but something in his expression must have given his true feelings away, for Ryan burst out into laughter. "I take it you disagree with the good father?"

Mpumelelo laughed too, shame-facedly. "Well, some of the conclusions he draws do seem a little far-fetched. And I also think he is writing from the perspective of a missionary. Either they are Christian and civilized or they are heathen and savage."

Ryan nodded. "And you propose to be less missionary in your approach."

"I hope to be, yes."

The captain said nothing, but sipped his drink in silence, looking out at the garden. Suddenly he stiffened. There was a very slight movement in the bushes near the fence marking the boundary of the compound.

Mpumelelo, noticing nothing, turned to Ryan. "Oh, captain," he began, but Ryan held up a hand, never taking his eyes off the garden.

"What is it?" Mpumelelo breathed, alarmed.

Ryan suddenly relaxed, and at the same time, a brown, cheerful looking man appeared as if from nowhere in front of them. He sprang up, laughing, onto the verandah.

Mpumelelo stared in surprise, for the man was no more than four feet tall.

"Greetings, Mangese!" Ryan said, getting up and offering the man his chair.

"Oh, Mobali Molai, a great tragedy has befallen the BaMbuti! I ran all the way, and I am so tired and hungry!" the man cried, beginning to weep as he spoke.

Mpumelelo was also on his feet, and he looked with alarm at both the others. He had thought that his mastery of the Mbuti language was more than enough to conduct his research, but, as so many of those who have learnt languages from books know, he was just realizing that the spoken language had a thousand small inflections impossible to convey on paper.

Unperturbed, Ryan fetched a drink for the pygmy, and sent the corporal out to bring some food. Until he had eaten and drunk his fill, the pygmy said nothing. Ryan told Mpumelelo that his name was Machenge, Mangese being a term of respect.

"Alright, Mangese," Ryan began, once he was done eating, "you can tell me what this great tragedy is."

At the reminder, Machenge began weeping again. "My brothers, my mothers, all captured," he sobbed.

"Captured?" Ryan asked, suddenly alert. "Who captured them?"

"The evil woman," Machenge said. "We thought it would be a fun game, a good trick to play. She told us it was for a short time; but then when we wanted to go back to the forest she trapped us. She has killed the son of my sister!" At this, he broke out into a storm of tears.

Ryan was now deadly serious. "Machenge, we cannot do anything until you tell us the full story. Now begin at the start and tell me all."

Wiping his tears, the man started.

"It was a while ago, we went to our village near the savages. While we were there, the savages brought a woman into the area, and she told us there was some work that we could do, easy work and we could earn a lot of tobacco and food. Some of us didn't want to go, we wanted to get back to the forest, but those young men thought it would be fine to work like the savages. Two families stayed back, and went to the forest to join another band, but the others, we went with the woman. And the work was hard. She made us crawl into the earth, into tiny holes, and like animals we had to dig out rocks and give them to her wicked servants, who hit us and beat us. They hit me, a grown man, in front of everyone. And when we sang, they beat us more. When we couldn't find rocks, they beat us. When we asked to go hunting, they beat us. When we said we didn't have enough food, they beat us."

"Why couldn't you leave?" Ryan asked, when Machenge stopped for breath.

"She locked us inside an iron hut at night. My sister's son tried to go back to the forest in the day time, and the woman's wicked servants took their guns and shot him as if he were an antelope. My sister has gone mad, and there is no more singing. The forest has deserted us," wailed Machenge.

"How did you escape?"

"I did not care if they killed me dead forever and ever. So I made for myself a small hole near the fence, and I hid there when everyone was going into the iron hut. Then I climbed over the fence and ran. I tried to find Ki-Gor, but he has left his home and no one knows where he has gone, so I came to you."

"Why is Ki-Gor not in his home?" asked Ryan, more of himself than of Machenge, but Machenge spoke up. "It is because the forest has forsaken the BaMbuti. We have done something wicked- perhaps in going with the evil woman in the first place- and so the forest has abandoned us. What use are BaMbutis whom the forest has abandoned?" He began crying again, while Ryan paced up and down the verandah, scowling horribly.

"This sounds like an illegal mining operation," he told Mpumelelo. "Ten to one this woman, whoever she is, is enslaving the pygmies to work the mines. We'll have to go and investigate this matter."

"I suppose now would be a bad time for me to carry out my research," Mpumelelo sighed. "And I would only get in your way if I were to come along."

To his surprise, Captain Ryan shook his head. "No, I think you could go ahead with it," he said. "This business sounds as if it only affects Machenge's band. You could make your way to another band of Mbuti, and carry out your research there. I will take a small platoon and try and investigate this mining thing. The only change to our plans is that I won't be able to accompany you as far as I said I would."

"If you're sure," began Mpumelelo, doubtfully.

"Yes," said Ryan. He turned to Machenge, who had finished crying and was eating the remainder of the food.

"I will go downstream, and try and find your band and the woman. You will have to give me directions."

"I can come with you," offered Machenge.

"No, you had best go back and try to find Ki-Gor. This problem sounds as if it will need all the help he can give."

"Ki-Gor," murmured Mpumelelo, "I can't remember that name in Father Schebesta's books."

Ryan looked at him strangely. "No, I don't think that name would have appeared there."

"But if he is a god..."

Machenge interrupted. "He is lord of the forest."

"Then Father Schebesta must surely have heard of some of the rituals surrounding him. Perhaps he is a regional god. This is very interesting." Mpumelelo produced a notebook and pencil and began scribbling in it.

Ryan looked like he was trying not to laugh. "What are you writing?" he asked.

"Just some notes. I must find out more about this Ki-Gor, and perhaps his significance in the Mbuti's rituals and religion."

Ryan openly laughed now, but when Mpumelelo looked surprised, he stopped. "Maybe Ki-Gor is not a god," he hazarded.

"Actually," said Mpumelelo, "I wrote my doctoral thesis on the gods of primitive people in the sub-Saharan region. Ki-Gor sounds as if he would fit the pattern of a jungle god. Yet there is nothing in the scholarly literature on him, which means that I shall be the first to write about him!"

Ryan was doubled up in laughter, but managed to summarize the discussion for Machenge's benefit. Machenge was actually rolling on the floor, crying with mirth.

"What's so funny?" Mpumelelo asked, a bit worried.

"Nothing, nothing," Ryan wiped his eyes. "I hope you will find Ki-Gor yourself."

Mpumelelo looked dubiously at him. "Is that some sort of blessing?" he asked.

The launch moved down the mighty Congo. Its waters lay still as the prow of the launch neatly divided it, leaving a creamy wake behind. Far on either side, Mpumelelo could make out the dense forest that marked its banks. They had been travelling for two days now, and Captain Ryan had told him that they should be nearing the dense forest in which the BaMbuti lived within the day.

On board the launch were Ryan, Mpumelelo, and the twenty man strong platoon which was accompanying Ryan to investigate the mines Machenge had spoken of. Machenge had set off after a brief rest to 'find Ki-Gor', which Mpumelelo assumed was the captain's way of telling him to get some rest and find a solution in religion.

The mood on the launch was pleasant; they had plenty to eat and although Ryan didn't want to waste time in investigating the mines, he did allow for a brief stop each evening, to cook and eat on land. Mpumelelo used these stops to accustom himself to the forest, which looked dense enough to him although everyone told him that they hadn't yet entered the forest proper.

It was mid-morning, and Mpumelelo was leaning on the railings of the deck, watching the trees slip past port. The bank to starboard was almost out of sight, just a dark haze on the horizon now and again. Captain Ryan joined him. "There's a place, near a BaMbuti village, a few miles ahead. We should reach there by this evening, and I will put you ashore there. The rest of us will proceed, and if you have any difficulties you can come back to the place I drop you off. We should pass that way in about three days' time, depending on what happens with this mines business."

"Do you continue up the Congo?" Mpumelelo asked.

"No, in fact we'll be swinging off presently- there's a small tributary which takes us to the heart of Ituri faster than going along the main river would."

As if on cue, the pilot swung the wheel round, and the launch slipped into a smaller river. This river was narrow, and the great trees on either side almost met in the middle, giving the river the illusion of a green tunnel. Huge vines hung down from the trees, and Mpumelelo sighed with joy. This was the Africa he had dreamt of while sitting in his grey lecture halls in Oxford. This was the Africa of the books he had read, the Africa he had represented in the student union. Never mind that his own childhood Africa had been thousands of miles away, in a luxurious Salisbury townhouse- *this* was the real Africa, Conrad's *Heart of Darkness* to the life.

The launch moved along, Mpumelelo and Ryan staying in companionable silence where they were. Suddenly Ryan stiffened.

"What is it?" Mpumelelo strained his eyes to see what Ryan was looking at. Instead of answering him, the captain barked out a low order to the pilot, who cut the engine and took the boat closer to the bank. Drifting along the bank, Mpumelelo suddenly caught sight of four BaMbuti emerging from the undergrowth.

"Mobali Molai! Save us! The BaMbuti are suffering!" they called, as the pilot dropped anchor.

"What is happening?" Ryan asked, making preparations to join them on land.

A rush of words hit him, as all BaMbuti tried to explain the story at once. Reaching the shore with Mpumelelo and one of the soldiers, Ryan sat down and held up a hand.

An old lady stepped forward. "I am Kimagi," she announced. "I will speak."

As concisely as possible, Kimagi repeated the story that Machenge had already told them. She said that she and the others had escaped three days after Machenge, and had been travelling ever since, trying to get to either Livingstone or Ki-Gor to raise the alarm and save the rest of the band.

"Alright," said Ryan, when she was done, "let's have a meal here and then decide what is to be done."

The group of escapees, which consisted of Kimagi, her teenage grandson and two small girls, sat down and began the meal with alacrity.

"I am taking these soldiers to investigate the mines," Ryan told them, "and Machenge has already gone on to find Ki-Gor. I think that the best thing for you to do is to travel on and find another band of BaMbuti. I will send word when I know more of what is happening."

"You had best take one of us, to show you the way," Kimagi suggested.

"I will take your grandson," Ryan decided. "You should be in charge of these children."

Kimagi acquiesced.

"Are you not afraid to travel without a male escort, especially since that evil woman is still in the jungle?" Mpumelelo asked, haltingly.

Ryan hid a smile. Kimagi snorted derisively. "Now that I am in the forest again, I can hide from any savage who tries to find me."

"We know that you can take care of yourself and these children, but will you as a favor to me take this man as well?" Ryan asked.

Kimagi looked doubtfully at Mpumelelo.

"Can he walk in the forest?" she asked.

"I don't think so, but he will learn," Ryan said.

Kimagi made a face. "We shall see. Alright, I will take him."

Ryan stood up. "Then we will go on our way, and leave you to go yours."

Kimagi also stood up and nodded gravely. "And let us hope that Machenge finds Ki-Gor and brings him back to save us."

As the sound of the launch's engine faded away, and only the usual jungle sounds and the river were heard, Mpumelelo made up his mind to ask Kimagi more about this Ki-Gor.

Kimagi turned to Mpumelelo. "Let's go. Stay close behind me."

Immediately she turned and plunged off into the bushes, through a gap that Mpumelelo would never have noticed on his own, or if he had, would have dismissed it as a gap made by and for wild pigs- not something that a human being could ever fit through. Yet to his amazement, once he had swallowed his trepidation, bent over double, and followed Kimagi, he found that it soon widened. What followed next was a wild run through the undergrowth, Mpumelelo struggling to keep his satchel with his scanty supplies over his shoulder. At times, even Kimagi was forced to stoop and run, and then Mpumelelo found himself crawling on hands and knees, but he somehow managed to keep up. He wondered at the incredible speed of the BaMbuti, at the little girls who almost danced ahead, coming back every few minutes to maintain contact with Kimagi more as if they were on a picnic in an open meadow than if they were fleeing for their lives through the densest undergrowth Mpumelelo had ever seen. Now he realized something, that although in the outside world of tall people, the BaMbuti's stature was a defect, inside their forest world it was essential to their speed and ease of passage.

At last, Kimagi turned. "Why are you so slow?"

Mpumelelo crouched down, panting hard, trying to readjust his satchel strap. "I- I thought that was fast!" he yelped.

Kimagi found this funny, and she began laughing until tears streamed from her eyes. Then suddenly awakening to the volume of sound she was making, she stopped abruptly. "It is alright for a savage," she said, generously, "but we will go a little faster in this next bit and then we'll reach the forest itself, so you

*What followed next was a wild run through the undergrowth.*

will be able to walk."

Mpumelelo stared in dismay at her. "What do you mean, forest? What is this?"

Kimagi snorted with laughter, and began running again.

After some time, Mpumelelo understood what she meant. They suddenly came out of the undergrowth, and found themselves in the primeval forest, which had never been cut down and therefore had no undergrowth. As Kimagi had promised, Mpumelelo found this area much easier to travel in, having no need to run bent over.

They were proceeding along at breakneck speed when suddenly Kimagi held up a hand. "Silent," she ordered.

Mpumelelo tried to mask the sound of his heavy breathing. The two little girls seemed as if they had turned to stone.

"We need to get into a tree," Kimagi said, shoving the girls towards a big tree with vines hanging low. "There are savages approaching."

"What savages?" Mpumelelo asked, as he was also unceremoniously bundled off towards a tree.

"You will see. They may work for the evil woman, so keep quiet." Kimagi found her own tree, and began climbing it nimbly.

Mpumelelo laboriously climbed his tree, making more noise than Kimagi and the two girls, and he wedged himself in the first branches- which were much, much higher off the ground than any of the trees in his childhood garden had been. By the time he had settled himself, the BaMbuti had all but effaced themselves from the scene. It was only by carefully staring at the places that he knew they were hidden that Mpumelelo managed to locate them. They were all intently watching the faint trail below them, which Mpumelelo had thought didn't exist except in the memory of Kimagi, but now found that did have a clear mark.

After about ten minutes, two burly black men wearing green uniforms came into sight. The color of their uniforms afforded them some small camouflage against the trees, but they made a considerable amount of sound. They both had rifles slung over one shoulder, and they stopped near the trees the BaMbuti and Mpumelelo were in to converse in low tones.

Mpumelelo heard snatches of their speech and realized that they were Bantu people, BaNkutu if he had to make a guess. He was very intrigued when he realized that these were the people the BaMbuti referred to as savages. Although, upon reflection, Kimagi had applied that term to himself too so perhaps it was a blanket term for all non-forest dwellers. What they were doing this far inside the forest, he had no idea. All his study had shown him that the non-forest dwellers did not like the forest, and avoided it where possible.

From what he could hear, they were discussing how to find more BaMbuti.

"We need to get more, for somehow the number decreases," one said.

"If we could find the savage creatures then we could get more," the other swore, "but they never stay in one place! They can appear and disappear at will."

"If we shoot a few, perhaps the others will remain in one place long enough for us to capture them."

Both laughed raucously, but their laughing was somehow uneasy, and the stillness of the forest soon overcame them. Mpumelelo thought that beneath their bravado and swagger there was still a strong element of superstitious fear of the forest.

Mpumelelo's legs were cramping under him. He winced and tried to keep as still as possible. One of the men handed his rifle to the other and wandered away, presumably to relieve himself, and the other stared idly into space. The second soon joined him, and both of them began moving off.

Mpumelelo decided that he could risk moving his leg very slightly. His leg hit his satchel, and as if in slow motion, he saw the satchel strap break and the entire thing tumble off the branch to the floor. It seemed to take an age until the satchel fell down, and it became unfastened on the way, some of the books falling separately. Finally they all hit the ground.

The effect on the BaNkutu would have been amusing if Mpumelelo had been in the frame of mind to appreciate it. As the thud of the satchel happened behind them, they leaped into the air, and spinning around, fired their rifles.

The forest air stayed dead silent after the echoes of the rifle shots died away. The usual sounds stopped for a while, as birds and animals nearby seemed to hold their breath. Mpumelelo almost followed his satchel down in his fright, but managed to calm himself down and wipe his sweaty palms on his trousers. Then he realized that he would have to go down anyway, if only to give Kimagi and the girls the chance to escape. The BaNkutu, unused though they might be to the ways of the forest, were not stupid enough to expect almost-new, English-made satchels to fall out of tall trees without any human agency. They would look for someone, and if they didn't find someone, they would shoot into the trees. Mpumelelo licked his dry lips, and then called out in Nkutu.

"Don't shoot!" His voice, to his disgust, came out in a squeaky tone.

"Come out immediately!" the BaNkutu ordered.

Mpumelelo slowly climbed down the tree, half-expecting at every moment to feel a bullet in his body. It never came, and he reached the ground and turned to face the BaNkutu.

"Ho," one said. Mpumelelo had never heard anyone except particularly bad-ly-written penny dreadful villains say 'Ho', so he didn't quite know how to react.

"He is a black man," the man told his companion, as if the latter didn't have eyes to see.

Mpumelelo had initially planned on remaining silent and as alive as possible, but now something prompted him to speak. "Yes, I am a black man," he repeated in Nkutu. "What of it?" He used as authoritative a tone as he could muster.

The BaNkutu seemed taken aback. "Er, what are you doing here, so far in the forest?"

"I am a botanist. I research plants," Mpumelelo said, confidently.

"Is that why you were up the tree?" asked one man, apparently not falling completely for Mpumelelo's bluff.

"No, I heard you two coming along the trail and I saw your guns, and I thought I had better get out of the way before you arrived."

"Why is that? Why are you afraid of some men with guns?"

Mpumelelo licked his lips nervously, a gesture that was not feigned in the slightest. "Do you work for... the British?" he asked.

The BaNkutu looked at each other and sniggered. "We work for a Queen, not a King."

Mpumelelo forced his body to relax. He breathed a sigh of relief. "I- well, I couldn't get my paperwork to enter the area filled out in time. Those white men- they never want to let a black man do as he pleases." He trailed off. The men exchanged knowing looks with him.

"Oh, is that all?" one of them inquired. "Don't worry, we won't tell the British about this. But perhaps- you know, it is hard work to remember what one must forget about, and..."

Mpumelelo gave another sigh, not of relief this time, and started digging in his satchel for the few pound notes he had left from his passage from Lagos. Almost snatching the money from him, the two men left, not even throwing a glance back at him.

Mpumelelo waited until they were just out of earshot, and then, as if to himself, he spoke in the Mbuti language. "I feel like walking away a little bit. I hope nothing comes out of the trees until I have walked for some time and those men have also left the area."

He picked up his satchel, holding it under his arm, and started walking in what he hoped was the right direction. He had walked for what seemed like an interminable amount of time, and his arms were hurting, and his stomach was growling, when he smelt smoke.

Very suddenly, he came into a small clearing- still covered from the sky by the overhanging trees- in which Kimagi and the two girls were waiting. They had built a tiny fire, over which something was cooking. As Mpumelelo approached, one of the little girls held up a long piece of material to him.

"Thank you," he said, awkwardly, taking it from her. "What is it?" He turned it in his hands.

The little girls were very amused, and laughed very hard at his perplexity.

"It is a carrying band," Kimagi told him, taking the food off the fire. Mpumelelo now saw that it was a sort of mushroom stew. "For your broken bag."

"Oh, er, thank you," Mpumelelo sat down on a stone and tied it to his satchel. Kimagi brought him some food.

"Was it a good idea to light the fire?" Mpumelelo asked, concerned. "Maybe there are more BaNkutu around the place."

Kimagi snorted. "BaNkutu? What do those savages know of the forest?" But all the same, she told the little girls to douse the fire and scatter the ashes when they were done with their meal.

They set off again, and Mpumelele had just begun to be aware of the slowly fading light when Kimagi stopped. She stood in the trail for a long time, not speaking, but concentrating hard on something.

Finally Mpumelelo addressed her. "What is it?"

Kimagi turned to him with an adoring light in her eyes. "It is Ki-Gor," she breathed. "We are saved."

"And he is someone whom you have encountered before?" Mpumelelo asked.

"Not me myself, but many others from my band," Kimagi threw over her shoulder, impatiently.

"Have these others told you their experiences themselves?" the anthropologist asked, trying his best to scribble notes in his notebook as they went.

"Yes," Kimagi sounded vaguely confused, "and the son of my sister is in service to him."

*K- nephew is priest of Ki-Gor*, Mpumelelo scrawled in his notebook.

"Is he… the molimo?" Mpumelelo asked, tentatively, not sure how the old lady would react to his bringing up the sacred molimo.

Kimagi actually stopped in her tracks. "You know about the molimo?" she asked, surprised.

Mpumelelo nodded. She set off again. "Ki-Gor is not the molimo. The molimo- well, you will find that out later. Ki-Gor is not a sacred thing like that."

"But Machenge told us that Ki-Gor was the Lord of the Jungle?" Mpumelelo asked, breathlessly, putting his notebook back in his satchel as they scrambled over a series of rocks. On the other side was a fast-tumbling jungle stream.

"Yes, he is, in a way," Kimagi said. "Follow me, but be careful. This stream is fast if you miss the right stones." The interrogation ceased for a while as they forded the river.

They reached the other side, and suddenly Kimagi gave a shout of joy and pointed at a still-steaming pile of elephant dung.

"Ki-Gor has passed this way not long ago!"

Wondering now whether Ki-Gor was an elephant, a Hathi-like figure, Mpumelelo asked, "Who IS this Ki-Gor?" He was more mystified than ever, and paused to inspect the elephant dung in case it was different from other elephant dung.

"Who wants to know?" came a deep voice, and Mpumelelo looked up to see the most confusing sight he had ever seen.

He had been hearing of Ki-Gor for the past three days, and he had never thought that Ki-Gor was someone who could be seen, and even if he had thought that Ki-Gor had an earthly manifestation or avatar, he had not envisioned anything like the figure standing in front of him. Yet his identity was left in no doubt, for Kimagi and the two children immediately cried out his name and rushed towards him.

On the trail in front of Mpumelelo stood a veritable giant of a man, tall and broad, with startlingly blond hair framing his deeply-tanned face. He wore nothing but a leopard-skin loin cloth, leaving his astonishing muscular development on full display. He wore a plain sword at his hip and a longbow and quiver of arrows on his back. Mpumelelo stared open-mouthed at him for a good while, taking in every detail of the man's appearance.

Ki-Gor was apparently doing the same, for when he spoke again, it was in English. "What is the problem?"

"Uh," said Mpumelelo, intelligently, and doing full credit to his many years of cloistered academic pursuits.

Ki-Gor laughed, and turned to Kimagi. "What is wrong, grandmother?" he asked, in the Mbuti language again.

"Oh, Ki-Gor, the BaMbuti are ruined! We are forever and ever dead!" she cried. "Also hungry," one of the children added.

Ki-Gor threw his head back and laughed. "Well, in that case, Kimagi shall tell us what has happened as we eat. Come along, who wants to ride on my shoulders?"

Mpumelelo had a distinct feeling of being in a dream as he walked in a strange parade into the camp of Ki-Gor. First, the diminutive pygmy lady who had guided him on the most strenuous journey of his life, then the blond, European-featured 'lord of the jungle' with two children on his shoulders, and finally the bedraggled and exhausted Mpumelelo Matthias, PhD (Anthropology). As they entered the clearing in which Ki-Gor had camped, the children and Kimagi ran to another pygmy, who greeted them ecstatically. Ki-Gor crossed to the cooking fires and spoke to a man attending the cooking pots. Two tall, well-made men with wicked-looking weapons glanced at Mpumele- lo- he estimated them to be Masa'i, although what Masa'i should be doing this far inside the forest he hadn't the foggiest idea. But Mpumelelo's eyes were drawn automatically to a figure on the far side of the clearing, a figure which was approaching him with a smile- a figure he had not thought to see in the whole 25,000 square miles of the Ituri- a white woman. Next to her was a tall, well-built black man, wearing the clothes of a Masa'i warrior, yet looking dif- ferent to the others. Mpumelelo paid no attention to him, however.

"Are you here with Kimagi?" the woman asked in English, coming up to Mpumelelo.

"Mmm," said Mpumelelo, unable to form coherent thoughts, let alone ex- press them verbally.

The woman laughed. "I am Helene, Ki-Gor's wife," she held out her hand.

"Mmm-Mpumelelo Matthias," he managed, finally, shaking her hand.

"Oh, from- is it South Africa, or Rhodesia?" Helene asked, her head to one side.

"Rhodesia."

"Oh, how nice! I have an uncle who lived there, and I remember visiting him once as a child. In Salisbury, that was," she said.

"That's where I'm from," Mpumelelo volunteered.

"What a coincidence," beamed Helene. "Come, Ki-Gor has just sorted out the meal. Let's go and listen to what Kimagi has to tell us."

"Oh," said Mpumelelo, remembering the mines. "It's not good. There's some- thing bad going on."

*It's not good. There's something bad going on,* a voice mocked him in his head, he, Mpumelelo, who had won an award for his oration at Oxford!

Helene didn't seem too concerned. "Ki-Gor will be able to sort it out, I ex- pect." She led him to where everyone was sitting down in a circle.

As they ate, night fell, and Kimagi's story of the mines fell on very attentive ears.

Ki-Gor listened to the whole in silence. Then he requested Mpumelelo to tell him what he knew, and then he thought.

Finally, he turned to N'geeso, Kimagi's nephew. "What do you think?"

N'geeso shrugged. "It is bad," he said, simply. "I am ready when you are, to fight."

Ki-Gor stared into the fire.

"Kimagi, will you take the children back to another band? They will be in danger's way if they remain here." He made the suggestion as a formal request.

Kimagi bowed her head. "I will do that."

"And what will you do, Dr. Matthias?" Ki-Gor asked, turning to look at Mpumelelo.

"Oh- it's Mpumelelo," the anthropologist said, awkwardly. "And I would like to go with Kimagi and the children, and join the other BaMbuti band."

"You want to get on with your work instead of coming with us?" Ki-Gor asked, mildly.

"I don't think that I'd be much help staying here," Mpumelelo pointed out, "everyone seems to be able to get around this forest much better than I can, and I have never used a weapon in my life."

"So you will go with the women and children," Ki-Gor mused, "and..."

"I beg your pardon," Mpumelelo sounded stiff, "but I don't quite like your tone of voice. I thought that by going with Kimagi I would be increasing your chances in a fight, since I would very probably be a liability if it came to violence."

Ki-Gor seemed surprised, and opened his mouth to retort, but Mpumelelo saw Helene place her hand on his arm and murmur something to him. "Very well," said Ki-Gor, "we can discuss this further tomorrow. Kimagi and the children will travel with us as far as the crossing of the two streams, and then they will head off towards the other bands while we make all haste to the mines."

No one had anything to add to this plan, and soon the fire was banked for the night and everyone curled up to sleep around it. Mpumelelo found the ground harder than even the rough rope hammocks of the launch, but his tired joints and aching muscles conspired to send him to sleep as soon as he had closed his eyes.

After they had washed sketchily at a stream and eaten some food the next morning, Ki-Gor approached Mpumelelo. The Masa'i who had been near Helene the previous night came with him.

"Mpumelelo, good morning," said Ki-Gor, easily. Mpumelelo felt embarrassed at the thought of his outburst the previous night.

"Good morning," he replied courteously. "Er, about my decision..."

Ki-Gor held up a hand. "No, I understand, if you want to go on and join the BaMbuti you are of course welcome to do so."

Mpumelelo was relieved. "It's just that- I have never fought, and I am not sure what would be expected of me. I feel that I would be better off doing the work I came here to do."

"I don't think that you will find normal conditions," Ki-Gor warned. "All of the BaMbuti bands are bound to be disturbed by this woman at the mines. And it doesn't make sense to me that you would go off without a care when the very people you came here to study are in danger."

The Masa'i laid a hand on Ki-Gor's arm. Ki-Gor took a breath and then shrugged. "I apologize. It is your decision, Dr. Matthias."

Mpumelelo understood the sting in Ki-Gor's use of his title, but rather than escalate the matter, simply inclined his head.

"The real question is, what's our plan for today?" asked the Masa'i, and Mpumelelo was startled. From the mouth of this man, a full warrior, came the nasal twang of the American. The night before, he had only spoken Masa'i or Mbuti, and his accent had been pure Africa. This morning, however, in English, he had a broad American accent.

"This is N'geeso's show," Ki-Gor said. "He will lead the way and tell us what exactly will happen. I expect we will arrive at the place where two streams cross sometime in the afternoon today, so then you, Dr. Matthias, and Kimagi and the children can leave us for the BaMbuti village. From then on, it will be up to N'geeso. Tembu George, if you could call him here he can give us any directions."

Mpumelelo only half took in the words he said, instead musing on the irony that, out of the three men, only Ki-Gor, the white man, should have an African accent when speaking English.

Tembu George went off to call N'geeso, and Mpumelelo was left alone with the self-styled Lord of the Jungle. He was conscious of a feeling of dislike towards the man, so big and brawny, so self-assured. All things Mpumelelo would never be. Strangely enough, it never occurred to Mpumelelo to judge him on the basis of his race- he knew too many white Africans to be surprised that one could know the Congo and its people as intimately as Ki-Gor did. No, what Mpumelelo felt was envy and frustration- how could this man fit in so well, be accepted by everyone, when he himself had always struggled? In Oxford, he was considered an anomaly. He knew very well that some of his colleagues regarded him as incapable, that when he travelled in the trains people assumed he was a menial worker, and that he would never exactly be given the full respect of a university don. In Salisbury (not that he had been there for some years, but he knew what it would be like) he was treated as an oddity, too Anglicized for the blacks and too black for the Anglos. Here, in the Congo, he felt that at last he was on ground that was at least neutral, and he had been feeling more comfortable than he had for some years- only to have it all spoiled by this man whom everybody loved. But who apparently disliked him, just because he was a non-violent character.

*What Mpumelelo felt was envy and frustration.*

Ki-Gor had also been studiously avoiding Mpumelelo's gaze, and both were relieved when Tembu George and Ngeeso came back. It was a funny sight, the big Masa'i and the small Mbuti, practically arm in arm except for their major discrepancy in height.

"We should start immediately," Ngeeso announced. "And no fires will be lit from now until we arrive at the mines."

"When will that be?" Tembu George rumbled.

"Tomorrow, perhaps after nightfall. We can launch our attack in the night, when everyone will be sleeping and not expect it. I will rouse the BaMbuti beforehand, and…" Ngeeso suddenly stopped explaining, and with a sense of dismay, Mpumelelo realized that it was because of him. Ki-Gor had made some signal to the Mbuti.

"We will go into the plan in greater detail tomorrow morning," Ki-Gor said, with an air of finality. "Ngeeso, give the order to march."

On the march, which was thankfully at a slower pace than the BaMbuti's headlong rush through the undergrowth, Mpumelelo was given the chance to renew his acquaintance with Helene, and make new acquaintance with Marmo, the elephant.

They trekked through the forest the whole morning, Ngeeso leading the way. The party made as little noise as was possible. Mpumelelo, despite having managed to keep up with the BaMbuti the previous day, found to his disgust that the exhaustion was now kicking in and he found it hard to keep up even with the tail of the procession. Helene walked next to him, not so much out of a desire to keep him company as to make sure he kept up with the rest of the party.

"Were you also born in Africa?" Mpumelelo asked her, trying to sound as if he had wind enough to spare for a conversation.

Helene seemed amused. "No, I was born in Boston. I came here only as an adult."

"Oh," Mpumelelo couldn't think of anything to say to this, so he remained silent.

After a while, Helene asked him about his work, and Mpumelelo, warming up to his topic, showed the ability to explain concepts and theories clearly yet not condescendingly, which had made him a favorite with his students. Helene asked intelligent questions, and Mpumelelo finally acquitted himself well. Then she turned the topic to that of the BaMbuti.

"I want," began Mpumelelo, speaking softly, "to write the most comprehensive study of the BaMbuti people and their culture that has so far been written."

"So, academic glory?" Mpumelelo looked up with a slight frown as Ki-Gor dropped behind to join their conversation.

"I suppose that's part of it," Mpumelelo admitted, keeping his temper in check, "but I also want to…I believe I'm just passionately interested in people. I want to experience at first-hand how the BaMbuti live."

Ki-Gor started to say something but then changed his mind.

Helene threw him a warning glance and then spoke. "Don't you think you can do something more for the BaMbuti?"

"Like what?"

"Like maybe writing in the newspapers? Drawing some attention to their plight?" Helene hazarded.

"I thought that Ki-Gor would be able to sort this mines thing out easily?" Mpumelelo asked. "I didn't realize it was such a serious thing that would require public opinion to be swung around."

Helene sighed. "Well, I don't think…I hope that it won't last as long as it would take for an article to make its way into the papers. But still, don't you feel called to do something about this?"

Mpumelelo stopped walking and turned to face her squarely. "What can I do, Helene?" he asked, exasperated. "I've already told you, I can't fight. How can I possibly help sort out this issue?"

Ki-Gor spoke, finally. "You *can* fight, or help to fight. You can at least keep guard over Marmo and any injured while we fight."

"No, I cannot," said Mpumelelo. "I can accompany Kimagi and the children. Other than that I cannot. What do I do if someone attacks the injured? I cannot kill."

"Why do you want so badly to be away out of danger? Is it that you are scared? Are you a coward?" Ki-Gor asked, entirely without rancor, but curiously.

Mpumelelo felt his face heating up. "I am an anthropologist! Anthropologists cannot influence or change the ways their subjects work! It's unethical, and it negatively affects their perceptions and biases! I refuse to relinquish hold of my lifelong dream just to join in some primitive fight with you and your gang of forest hoodlums!"

Ki-Gor's eyebrows went up. Before he could respond, however, a scream rent the air up ahead of them. In a bound, Ki-Gor had left them and was running up the trail, unsheathing his sword as he did so.

"Stay behind me," Helene hissed, and Mpumelelo noticed that she too had drawn a blade; in her case, a small, wicked-looking knife.

"What is it?" he breathed, fearfully. Marmo's bulk, just ahead of them, blocked their view of the rest of the group. After that one scream, no further sound came from the group ahead of the elephant.

Helene shrugged and said nothing, but her eyes scanned the surrounding forest keenly.

Mpumelelo tightened the bark strap of his satchel, and his salivary glands had just started working again when Helene tensed. In front of them, Marmo's ears flapped once, then twice. There was a sudden feeling of almost unbearable menace, and then Helene lunged sideways swiftly. For an instant, Mpumelelo thought that she was going to stab him, and then he was sent sprawling off the faint trail against the trunk of a tree. He was winded, but he had the unconscious realization that it was Helene's shoulder that had struck him rather than the blade of her knife. As he sprawled there, Helene threw herself after him, and the next moment, Marmo's tail went up, and making the most awful screaming sound Mpumelelo had ever heard, she turned right round and stampeded away, right over the spot where he and Helene had been standing. Streaking behind her, Mpumelelo caught a glimpse of a tawny form, and then the crashing sounds of the elephant receded. Before he could get his breath back, Mpumelelo saw Ki-Gor running after them, stopping only to make sure Helene hadn't been crushed by Marmo.

"What was that?" he gasped, clawing his way to his feet.

"Leopard," said Helene, with clenched teeth. "Someone must have been savaged. They'll need our help." She began running along the trail to the knot of people who stood a few yards away.

"Do you know any first aid?" she threw, over her shoulder.

"A little," Mpumelelo answered, afraid to see the damage done by the leopard, yet knowing he had to do what he could.

They burst through the knot of warriors to where Kimagi knelt on the ground, holding one of the children. The child's side was soaked in blood.

"What happened?" Helene rapped out, shoving people back to give the child air.

"Her arm," Tembu George said, somberly.

Kimagi had already moved the child's arm away from her body, revealing the large and gory slash from elbow to wrist. The child, mercifully, had fainted, making it a little easier for the first aid givers.

"She threw up her arm to protect her face," Kimagi explained, in a soft whisper.

"Was she away from the trail?" Helene asked, as Mpumelelo carefully examined the wound.

"No, she was right here. You're doing it wrong, I will attend to it," Kimagi said, breaking her own explanation off to address Mpumelelo.

Helene slipped into Kimagi's place, pillowing the child's head, and Tembu George took up the story as Kimagi went off to pick some leaves.

"She was with us. I took both children with me and we were behind Ngeeso, but within sight of the ones behind us. This leopard sprang out of the trees, almost from nowhere and fortunately the child had presence of mind to protect her face. Better to lose an arm than an eye," Tembu George said, macabrely.

"She will lose nothing but a little blood," Kimagi announced serenely, rejoining them. She handed some leaves to Mpumelelo, adding another type of leaves from the pouch around her waist. "Chew these and give me the paste," she ordered.

Mpumelelo was taken aback, but did as he was told. The leaves tasted terrible, and he quailed to think of the vast quantity of blood Kimagi would require before she would refer to it as more than 'a little'.

He spat the green gunk out into Kimagi's outstretched hand, and she slapped it thickly on the child's arm.

"We need more." She handed more leaves to Mpumelelo.

Helene grinned at him in sympathy as he chewed the new batch.

Tembu George spoke. "I hope Ki-Gor kills the leopard."

Helene glanced up at him. "He does not normally kill for the sake of killing," she pointed out, "and this animal was merely defending itself against a perceived threat."

Tembu George shook his head. "This animal deliberately attacked. Or, was sent to attack."

"Nonsense," said Helene, briskly, "who could send a forest leopard to attack?"

"But this wasn't an ordinary forest leopard," Tembu George insisted. "It had a diamond-encrusted collar."

Ki-Gor returned to camp, leading Marmo. The elephant had a few scratches on her back, but was otherwise unharmed. The injured child had woken from her faint, and sat with the other child in a corner, being fed a stew by their concerned uncle, N'geeso.

Satisfied that the child was not in danger, Ki-Gor turned to Helene. "I found Marmo, but had to let the leopard go. He'd chased her into a thicket where she got caught fast and scratched by thorns. I had to shoot an arrow at him before he would leave her, but it merely scratched his leg."

"Tembu George thinks the leopard was set on us," Helene told him.

Ki-Gor glanced over at Tembu George, looking distracted. "I saw that too. What do you make of it?"

Tembu George shrugged his powerful shoulders and remained silent.

"It is the woman from the mines," Kimagi said.

Everyone turned to look at her. "What?" asked Ki-Gor, finding his voice after a pause.

"I didn't see her. She didn't come to the house where we were, but someone who went out said that she kept two leopards, bad-tempered, nasty brutes, in her house."

"Why didn't you mention this before, when Tembu George told us he'd seen the collar?" Helene demanded.

"No one asked me," Kimagi shrugged, and she turned away to help herself to some food.

"This means we are closer to the mines than we thought," Tembu George said, somberly. "Hey, N'geeso, come here. We'll have to think of an alternate plan."

N'geeso took no notice until the children had finished eating, then he sauntered over.

"We shall have to go in and fight tonight."

"What about Kimagi and the children?" Ki-Gor asked.

"We will go to the nearest camp. Mpumelelo can come with us," Kimagi was firm.

"Then you shall have to leave now," Ki-Gor said, "but I am not happy to send you alone with those leopards around."

"Now we know that there are leopards," Kimagi pointed out, "so we will be more careful. Besides, the leopards were sent for you. You will be the ones travelling further into the evil woman's territory, while we make our way away from it."

Ki-Gor exchanged glances with N'geeso.

"Alright," he gave in, finally. "Mpumelelo will travel with you. But you must leave now, before the leopard returns to her and she sends another one."

Immediately packing their few belongings, the BaMbuti were ready to leave by the time Mpumelelo got himself together. With Kimgai carrying the injured child on her hip, they soon plunged off down a tiny track.

Ki-Gor watched them going. Then he turned to Helene and spoke softly, his words intended only for her.

"I must go into the mining camp."

"Not alone?" Helene asked, worried.

"I will go with him," N'geeso volunteered, shamelessly eavesdropping although Tembu George had taken a step away to avoid hearing.

"Alright, N'geeso shall go with me. But we need to see the setup of the camp before attacking. I have a plan; N'geeso shall join the BaMbuti inside their hut, and will let me in after dark. Then we'll try to get the captive BaMbuti roused up and shall attack the guards. At the same time, all of our men led by you and Tembu will attack the camp from the outside. With any luck, we'll soon overpower them and get out of there before daybreak."

"Good plan," N'geeso nodded, his eyes alight at the thought of a good fight. "We had better get moving."

Dusk saw the party encamped in a clearing. N'geeso, acting as scout, had travelled a mile ahead and returned with the news that the mining camp was located at the bottom of a small hill. It was decided that he and Ki-Gor would set out immediately, with the others remaining where they were. Lookouts posted at intervals closer to the camp would pass along any signals, including the one to attack.

Ki-Gor took Helene's hands in his big ones. "We will give the signal within two hours," he told her. Looking over her head at Tembu George, he nodded gravely at him. "If you don't hear anything by then, send one person to find out what has happened." Tembu George nodded somberly.

Helene watched them disappear into the gathering darkness, the tall, broad figure of her husband and the tiny one of the Mbuti. She breathed a prayer for their safety, and then turned back to join Tembu George in the readying of all weapons.

Ki-Gor and N'geeso walked silently through the night. They took turns leading, allowing the one following to catch a respite from the constant strain of peering through the night. In a short while, they reached the top of the hill. The hill, cloaked in trees and undergrowth, sloped downwards to a large clearing. The clearing was bisected by a swiftly-flowing river, which formed a natural boundary to the mining camp. Ki-Gor's keen eye noticed a fence running into the river from the camp; glancing the other way he saw another. He followed it with his eye to where it disappeared below him. Touching N'geeso's arm, he pointed, and the Mbuti understood that the fence probably ran along the bottom of the hill, enclosing the camp securely. The river was now in full spate, meaning that there could be no escape from that side.

Within the camp itself were two large huts made of tin. One was completely in darkness, the other showed yellow light from the cracks between walls and roof. Scattered around the rest of the camp were smaller huts, including two structures without walls which enclosed what looked like wells. Ki-Gor assumed that these were the mineshafts. There were also large pieces of machinery lying around, looking like grotesque monsters.

N'geeso gestured towards the large hut in darkness. Ki-Gor nodded. He too expected to find the BaMbuti inside that hut. Pausing only long enough to memorize the layout of the camp, the two men plunged silently down the hillside.

They reached the edge of the fence, and here both were glad they had taken the time to spot it. It was well-camouflaged among the trees and undergrowth, and if they hadn't known it was there they might have walked straight into it.

N'geeso started towards it, but Ki-Gor roughly thrust him back. His sharp eyes had seen a large box affixed to one of the fence posts.

"What is it?" breathed N'geeso, confused.

In reply, Ki-Gor stooped, picked up a stick, and threw it at the top wire of the fence. Nothing happened.

"Is it a trap?" N'geeso asked.

"It is, I think, electricity," Ki-Gor answered. "It will sting you or maybe kill you if you touch it."

"How do we get over?" N'geeso looked around for another way through the fence.

"Perhaps we can dig under it?" Ki-Gor knelt and began shifting the earth beneath the fence. Very soon, he had a hole large enough for N'geeso to go through.

"If you tell me how to stop the stinging thing, I can do it," N'geeso volunteered. Ki-Gor agreed, realizing how much time would be wasted in both enlarging the hole enough for his own use and in trying to take the BaMbuti out through one hole. Disabling the electric fence now would save much time later.

Soon, N'geeso was opening the box on the fencepost. Unsure of what to do exactly, Ki-Gor instructed him to cut all the wires inside using his stone arrowhead. A startling shower of blue sparks resulted, which fortunately attracted no attention. Then, hesitantly, Ki-Gor reached out and touched the wire. Nothing happened, and with a bound, the lord of the jungle was inside the fence.

"Get into the hut and rouse the BaMbuti," he told N'geeso. "I will find out more about this camp."

Ki-Gor slipped silently around the dark hut, leaving N'geeso to find his way inside. He went past the mineshafts and towards the big lighted hut, from which he could hear the sounds of merriment. He was near one end when a large door was suddenly flung open, throwing a wide swath of light across the ground, ending almost at his feet. In the instant before it touched him, Ki-Gor had twisted and leapt, agile as any cat, behind one of the pieces of machinery which littered the area.

Someone stood in the doorway, speaking to those behind them. Then they turned, and Ki-Gor saw that it was a woman who stood silhouetted against the light. She wore a flowing robe, and from either hand she held a leash; the end of each was attached to the jeweled collar of a magnificent leopard. While the woman spoke, the leopards scented Ki-Gor, and the one which bore the marks of his arrow snarled.

"What is it, my darlings?" the woman spoke to them, and she glanced around blindly in the dark.

Ki-Gor scanned the area quickly to confirm he was where he thought he was, and then turned his eyes back to the leopards just in time to see the woman begin to unclip the leash of the uninjured animal.

"Go hunting, my sweet, if you think one of those nasty pygmies are out again." She patted it on its flank as it shot straight towards Ki-Gor.

Ki-Gor had no time to watch the reaction of the woman as he took to his heels in the direction of the mineshaft furthest away from the BaMbuti's hut. The leopard ran silently after him, yet Ki-Gor dared not look behind for fear of tripping. Finally, he reached the mineshaft and whipped his knife out as he turned to face the leopard, keeping the shaft behind him.

The leopard seemed surprised that he had stopped, and as a result, mistimed its leap. Ki-Gor stayed still, ducking only at the very last moment. The leopard, unable to stop itself, went over his shoulder to the edge of the shaft, clawing at the stone edge to prevent itself from going over. Ki-Gor immediately shoved it, and with a terrible cry the leopard went over the edge. Ordinarily, he would have made sure the animal was dead without unnecessary suffering, but today Ki-Gor had no time to spare. He realized, from the lack of reaction in the camp, that the woman must have been turning away even as she unclipped the leopard, expecting it to return after killing the unfortunate escapee. He didn't think it would be very long before she noticed the failure of the cat to return, so he hurriedly loped off in the direction of the BaMbuti hut.

Before he was halfway there, a cry arose from the lighted hut. Without pausing to find out its cause, Ki-Gor threw caution to the wind and sprinted to the hut. Within seconds, he was inside, ready to take charge of the BaMbuti and lead them out. Inside the hut, however, he was faced with people lying down and sleeping. Only a few were awake, and N'geeso was almost dancing with impatience in front of these.

"What's wrong?" Ki-Gor rapped out.

"They are afraid to escape," N'geeso explained quickly. "These others went back to sleep saying they need strength to work tomorrow, if they are not to be beaten."

"We have very little time," Ki-Gor said, in an awful voice. The BaMbuti who were awake stirred slightly, and a few others woke up.

"Come on," said N'geeso, encouragingly, "Ki-Gor has come to save you!"

Two BaMbuti stood up, but it was too late. The door was flung open, and men with rifles stood outside. N'geeso darted over the Ki-Gor's side. "I'll take the ones to the right, and you can go left," he suggested, nocking an arrow to his bow.

Ki-Gor pushed his bow down. "There's too many," he said, gravely. "We'll have to risk capture rather than throw our lives away."

The other hut was very bright to be in. Ki-Gor and N'geeso, stripped of their weapons, were herded roughly inside it. The remaining leopard snarled at

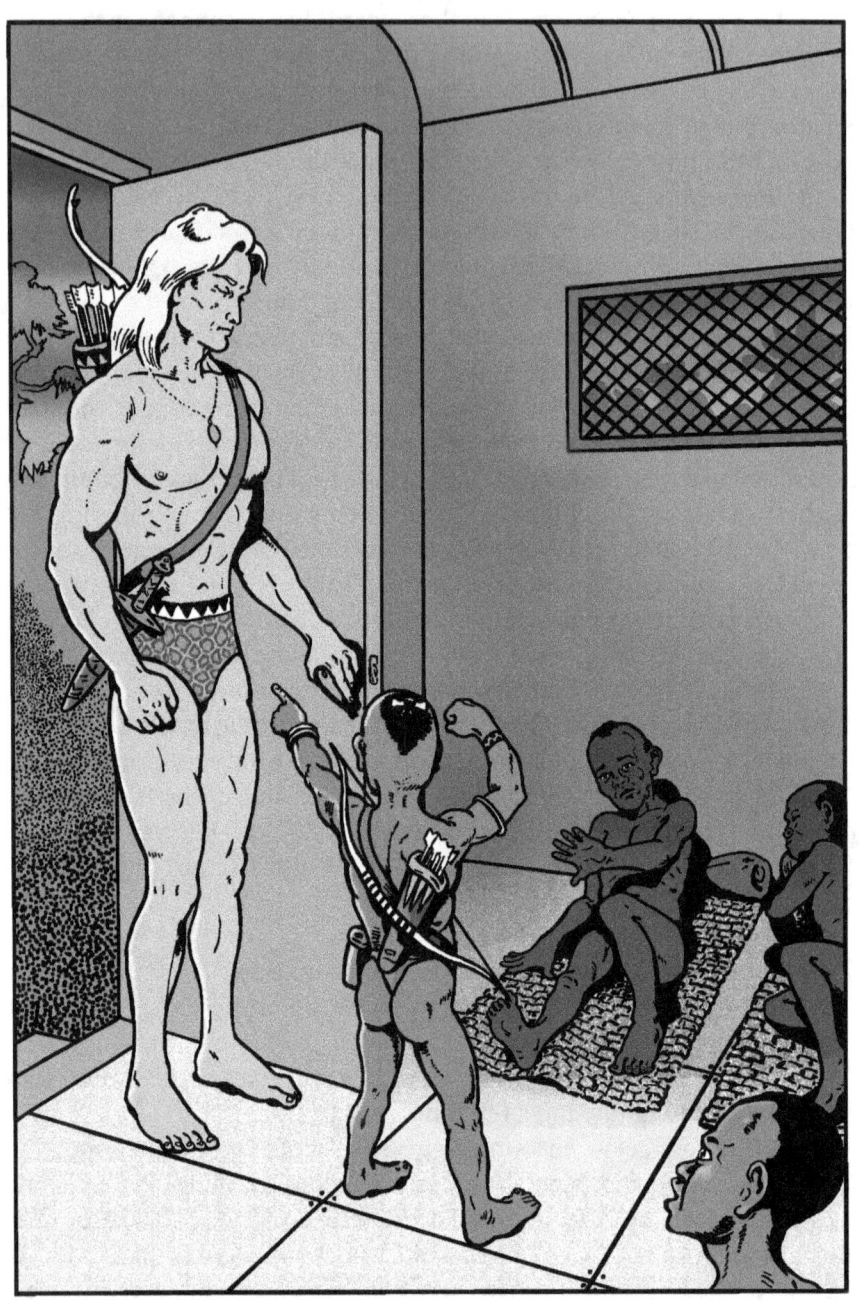

*"Come on! Ki-Gor has come to save you!"*

them, and the woman swept in behind it. Now for the first time Ki-Gor got a good look at her. To his surprise, he realized she was white. Dressed in a swirling white robe, she wore also a leopard skin cloak and heavy gold necklaces.

"Are these the ones?" she asked, to Ki-Gor's surprise in an English accent.

"They are the ones, O Queen," one of the BaNkutu guards said.

"This is… Ki-Gor, Lord of the Jungle?" she inquired, walking around the two prisoners. "And one of my pygmies, who has decided to escape?"

"It is he, O Queen," the guard replied. The Queen turned her full attention to Ki-Gor and N'geeso.

"What are you doing inside my camp?" the Queen asked, putting her head on one side like a curious bird of prey.

"What are you doing with all those BaMbuti?" Ki-Gor countered.

"As you are the trespasser here, I don't think you have any right to ask me questions," the Queen said, pleasantly.

"But as you are the criminal, I don't think I will answer any questions." Ki-Gor shrugged his massive shoulders.

The Queen frowned. "Let's see how long you can hold out when my guards get a bit more… persuasive," she purred. "Take him to the …chamber," she ordered. "And we will flog the pygmy at dawn, for daring to escape from my hut. Put him back with the other pygmies until then."

They dragged Ki-Gor off to one of the smaller huts. As they took him, he saw another guard taking N'geeso to the BaMbuti hut. Then the Queen swept into the hut behind them, and she closed the door with a final sound.

"I don't like this," Helene paced the clearing for the fifteenth time. "I think we should go and see what's happening."

"He said to give him two hours," Tembu George reminded her. "We could spoil his whole plan if we went early."

Just then, one of the lookouts who had been posted between the mining camp and the clearing burst in. "The camp is awake, and the guards are very active," he gasped.

"Ki-Gor?" Helene breathed.

"Couldn't see him."

Helene turned resolutely to Tembu George. "We must go and rescue him."

"First of all, Helene," Tembu George gently turned her to face him, "we must go to finish the job he started. The BaMbuti need rescuing much more than

Ki-Gor does. We go there to rescue them, and if we can rescue Ki-Gor at once, all the better."

Helene took a deep breath. "You are right," she said, simply. "Let's go."

The damp, cold darkness of the hour before dawn was upon the jungle as they crept down the hillside towards the camp. The small body of warriors was just behind them, at the crest of the hill, whence they could pour down in a flood if the need arose.

Some fortune led them close to the hole that N'geeso had dug; and rather than risk the fence, Helene crawled through.

"No way I can go through that," Tembu George said, looking with disdain at the small hole as Helene stood up and brushed dirt off her clothes. "Nor could Ki-Gor. I guess he jumped this fence, and that's what I'm going to do."

"But they must have had a reason for digging underneath," Helene protested. Tembu George ignored her, and stepping forward, gripped the fence.

Immediately he went into convulsions. His fingers gripped even tighter than before.

"Let go, let go!" Helene cried, not caring if her shouts attracted attention.

George somehow managed to release the wire, and fell to the ground senseless.

In a flash, Helene went back through the hole. She got a bad shock when she touched George's arm.

Not knowing what else to do, she crouched over him and stared at his chest to see if he was breathing. He soon opened his eyes, and looked disoriented at her.

Helene risked touching him again, and the shock was less this time.

"Wait here," she told him, "I'll get one of the lookouts to take you back to the clearing."

"You can't go...alone," George gasped.

"Nonsense," Helene snapped, and ran into the jungle.

Soon she was back with one of the lookouts, and as soon as she saw Tembu George sitting up, she slipped under the fence, took a deep breath, and started off.

She made her way to the first structure she could find, hoping it would provide her with a little screen from the guards. It was a tiny hut. Crouching behind it, Helene looked around to make sure of her bearings. Ahead of the hut were the two big huts, one of which was a hive of activity. The other one was silent, but four armed guards patrolled outside it. She was instantly sure that she had to somehow obtain access to that hut. The only problem was how.

Helene was still thinking when a sound from inside the hut she was crouching behind drew her attention.

"Tell us the truth!" a female voice said, followed by the sound of a slap.

Helene cautiously looked at the wall of the hut, but saw no window through which she could look.

There was no reply to the harsh voice, and Helene heard another smack.

A hot anger filled her. Whoever was inside the hut, Ki-Gor or not, was being interrogated harshly. Who were these people, who came into the jungle and tried to take it over for their own nefarious purposes?

She hit upon a sudden plan. Pursing her lips, she gave vent to the cry of a moorhen. It was the one bird she could imitate realistically, and there were no moorhens in this part of the jungle. She waited breathlessly, and then repeated the cry.

From inside the hut there came another sound now. "Alright, I'll talk," came the voice of her husband.

"Why are you here?" the insulting voice came again.

"Because of the BaMbuti inside the big hut," Ki-Gor said, his voice raised slightly louder than usual.

The soft thud of a fist landing on flesh made Helene even angrier, but she held her temper in check and stayed where she was.

"What do you want with them?" the interrogator asked.

"To rescue them!" Ki-Gor spat. "If you didn't have those electric fences they would be free by now."

He was trying to warn her about the fences, Helene realized, a wry smile on her face. Too bad they had already found out the hard way.

"They wouldn't be free," the female voice contradicted him, "because they are mine. I have put the fear of the jungle into them, and they will do everything I tell them. They will never leave this place."

"What do you want them for?" Ki-Gor asked.

"I am the interrogator," the voice reminded him, coldly, "but since you won't be leaving this place alive, you should know that I have found a certain diamond mine. The place was worked in ancient times, and the shafts and passages were built by small people. The normal sized BaNkutu cannot fit into them, as we found out after three got stuck and died. So I had no choice but to get these pygmies to work them."

"As your slaves," Ki-Gor snarled.

"Of course," the voice sounded amused. "Did you think I was going to pay them?"

"Who are you?" Ki-Gor asked.

"They call me Queen," the woman said. "And Queen I will be, when the diamonds I find have been all mined. You think you have a monopoly over the Congo? Well, Ki-Gor, I too can rule over the forest as well as you."

"I do not buy any power or position with riches or with fear," Ki-Gor's replied.

"So noble of you," the woman purred. "However, I do. The blacks will never say no to a white person, as I'm sure you've found out to your gain."

"I am African!"

"You are white. Don't pretend that the color of your skin has nothing to do with what you are, what you do in this forest."

Ki-Gor snarled. "I was born here. I have lived here all my life, and my people know that and they trust me because of it. The blood of the Congo runs in my veins. I am not some random person who came here and imposed my will on the people of the forest."

"And I am?" the Queen asked. "Well, Ki-Gor, perhaps you are right. But you know that we have divine right to rule over these savages. They don't know anything, and we are appointed by nature to wield authority over them. I am divinely ordained to be in charge of this part of the jungle, just as you are appointed to rule your part of it."

"I am not divinely appointed. And neither are you. My people chose me to lead them, and you use force and violence to rule over the people here. There is no love between you and them, as there is between me and my people. You think because you are white you have some mysterious power over the people of the forest. You are wrong!"

"Ki-Gor- that's what they call you, isn't it? I understand only that you are jealous that a woman should try to do what you have already done; bent the will of the people to your own benefit."

"You will never understand the bond I have with my people. I will not stand by and allow you to make them into slaves again."

"They will be my slaves for just as long as I wish them to," the woman snapped.

"They will be free," Ki-Gor's voice seemed to be growing fainter, and Helene worried that he was badly hurt.

"Who will free them now that Ki-Gor, Lord of the Jungle, is tied up and a bloody mess inside this hut?" The woman laughed pleasantly. Helene gritted her teeth, and then forced herself to move.

The fence was electric, so her first task would be to find the source of power and turn it off. She made her way, crouching and running, between the cover afforded by the machinery and little huts until she reached the perimeter fence. Working her way along the fence towards the hill, she looked at each little box on the posts. Disabling each one individually would take far too long. She was inspecting one when a shadow fell on her, and from the corner of her eye she saw someone looming up near her. Panicking, she whipped around with her hands ready to scratch and buy her even a little time. Hands caught her own wrists, but before she could bring her knee up and kick the person, she recognized the face of Tembu George.

"How did you come in?" she whispered.

"Dug the hole a bit more," he explained. "What have you found?"

"Ki-Gor is in one of the small huts. A woman is interrogating him. The BaMbuti are inside the big hut with the guards, and the fence is electric."

Tembu laughed softly, showing his white teeth. "I knew that last fact."

"Can you disable it?" Helene asked, urgently. "I will try and get the BaMbuti out."

Tembu didn't even answer, but began running cautiously along the fence, heading towards the river.

Helene also took off, making her way at a slower speed to where the BaMbuti's hut stood, with the four men still guarding it. She knew she wouldn't be able to take on all four men, so she tried to think of a distraction that would leave the coast clear for her to open the hut doors.

Just then, a small explosion shook the camp. A bright flare of light came from near the river, and then quickly subsided. Helene, though taken unawares, immediately assumed that Tembu George had had something to do with the explosion and prepared to take full use of the momentary distraction. The guards, however, had no idea what had happened and milled about in consternation. After a short discussion, three of them ran off towards the river, joining other men who were running in that direction. The sole remaining guard would provide no major obstacle to Helene, and she immediately ran to the side of the hut while the man was busy staring after his fellow guards. Moving silently and slowly, she maneuvered herself to a position just behind the guard, and then she struck at the base of his skull, a place N'geeso had showed her. N'geeso's suggestion had been to use a knife and so put her opponent permanently out of action, but Helene preferred the rounded end of the wooden knobkerrie she always carried. The results pleased her, as the man dropped like a stunned bear. He dropped so suddenly, in fact, that Helene worried she had killed him after all. She had no time to ascertain this, so she left him lying there and put her shoulder to the bar which lay across the big double doors. An almighty heave threw it free, and as she turned to drop it on the ground she saw a figure in a loose white robe leave the small hut that Ki-Gor had been in and rush towards her.

Helene barely had time to turn before the figure blew a whistle, a terrible, high-pitched sound that rang in Helene's ears.

The door of the other hut flew open, and as if in a bad dream, Helene saw a leopard with a jeweled collar charge towards her, belly down on the ground. She tightened her grip on the knobkerrie, and then she heard a low roaring sound. Thinking it was the blood rushing in her ears, she paid no attention to it, but suddenly, as the leopard closed the gap between them with frightening speed, she felt someone standing behind her.

"Get behind me, I'll handle this one," N'geeso said, and then the low roaring sound grew louder and Helene found herself stumbling behind the stocky pygmy as he hefted his spear and threw it at the leopard. Even before she saw the leopard fall, the spear tip in its heart, she was surrounded by BaMbuti pouring out of the hut behind her.

She saw the figure in white throw up its hands in frustration and annoyance, and then she saw the guards returning from the waterside, leveling their guns at the crowd of BaMbuti.

"Get them," N'geeso shrieked, pointing at the guards. But Helene saw that it was hopeless, that the BaMbuti were simply too few to overpower the guards. They were also weak from their long captivity, and she doubted whether they would be able to trek through the forest at night even without having to fight the well-fed and fire-armed BaNkutu. The BaMbuti still came out of the hut, children and old people last. Finally, Helene was behind all the BaMbuti. Still she heard the low roar come from behind her, and then a huge, splintering crash. She turned.

One entire section of the fence was down, and pouring over it were more BaMbuti; only these were healthy and well-armed. Helene stared in shock, and then caught sight of a tall figure among them, carrying a khaki satchel much the worse for wear. Mpumelelo waved at her, and then the new wave of BaMbuti swept past her. Hard on their heels came the rest of Ki-Gor's men, minus a very few who would be back at the clearing with the stores and Marmo.

The guards, who a minute ago had been leveling their rifles at the scrawny, ill-clad and cowed BaMbuti from the hut, now took one look at the swarms of rested and fighting mad newcomers and ran. They threw down their weapons as they did so, and the BaMbuti from the camp stood aside to let their friends from the forest take over the pursuit. Soon the guards had made it to the perimeter fence, and the BaMbuti chased them into the forest.

"Don't let them hurt them too much," Helene called, and N'geeso turned back and flashed a quick smile. "I can't stop them," he explained, "but things will be very unpleasant for the BaNkutu who don't leave the forest as soon as possible."

"Let the ones who were here go free into the forest," Helene said, and then she turned to see where the Queen had gone.

Now the sounds of the pursuit grew faint in the forest, and the slowest of the BaMbuti who had been in the camp were helping each other over the fence. Helene was alone in the centre of the camp, and she advanced slowly, her small hunting knife at the ready. Where was the Queen?

She thought she heard a small growling noise from the mine shaft on her left and turned sharply. Out of the corner of her eye she saw someone running, and when she looked to the right she saw she was too late. The Queen had reached one of the small huts. As Helene ran towards her, the Queen slammed open the door and then reappeared, dragging Ki-Gor out.

"I will kill him if you come closer," she said, calmly, looking at Helene. Helene stopped in her tracks.

Ki-Gor looked much the worse for wear, with blood half-dried on the side of his face and bruises elsewhere. He was dazed, and slowly raised his head to look at Helene. "Don't bargain with her," he said, weakly.

"You have to guarantee my safe passage out of the forest, or he dies," the Queen stated. She pulled a knife out and held it to Ki-Gor's throat.

"Alright," Helene said, resignedly. "Tell me what you want."

The Queen seemed surprised that she had agreed to hear her out so quickly. "An escort of you and Ki-Gor to the edge of the forest, and a promise of complete immunity afterwards."

"What's to keep us from making the promise and then breaking it once we have you as our prisoner?" Helene demanded.

The Queen was taken aback. It was clear that she hadn't thought this far. In the end she fell back upon a lame threat. "I have ways of making sure you don't."

Helene shrugged. "Alright, you have my word."

The Queen smiled wickedly. "Well, you had better tie my hands up or something. There's some strong rope over there near the mineshaft."

Helene glanced quickly to her left, and saw a coil of rope near the shaft. She turned back to the Queen, who gave her a guileless look. Something seemed wrong to Helene, but she couldn't figure what, so she turned and walked to the shaft.

As she was bending down to pick the rope up, the sense of foreboding intensified, and suddenly Ki-Gor shouted. "Helene! Look out!"

With a rush, the Queen was on her, and Helene felt a hot lash across the back of her upper arm. Quick as a flash, she turned to face the Queen, who held the knife across her body, trying to get another cut at Helene. Helene's eyes were drawn irresistibly to the knife, the blade of which was wet with her blood. Her arm was burning, but her fingers worked, and she kept her arms up to protect her head and body.

The Queen lunged again, and in an instant Helene knew that she was trying to push her down the shaft. She succeeded in pushing Helene off balance. Her upper body was bent back over the shaft, as her arms frantically pushed the Queen off. From the depths of the shaft, far below, a blood-curdling snarl drifted up. Helene, not knowing of Ki-Gor's affray with the leopard, had no idea what it was, but she did know that she didn't want to find out.

The Queen raised her knife, and in doing so, shifted her weight off Helene very slightly. Helene gave one last tremendous effort and rolled her body sideways. The Queen had already started her downwards swing, and the momentum carried her forwards and into the shaft. Appalled, Helene watched as the world seemed to slow down and the Queen toppled and then fell into the shaft with a despairing wail.

The snarls from below mingled with an awful shriek, and then the world went black and Helene fainted.

It was a jubilant party that sat around the fire when Helene recovered enough to join them. Captain Ryan and his men had landed minutes before, and Ki-Gor, his wounds bandaged, was regaling them with the story. Mpumelelo sat next to him, both men behaving like best friends, and Tembu George stood with N'geeso to one side. They looked at Helene, and she raised a hesitant eyebrow.

"She and the leopard killed each other," Tembu George said.

"And Captain Ryan's men will be rounding up the main BaNkutu guards with the help of the BaMbuti." N'geeso grinned.

"And everyone is happy, and the thing is over, and Mpumelelo will bother the BaMbuti for a while longer but nobody really minds."

Helene smiled. "And we can go back into the forest," she suggested. "Honey season is almost here."

**THE END**

# Writing Ki-Gor

**W**riting 'The Curse of the Queen' was really fun for me. I'd been reading John Drummond's Ki-Gor when I decided to write a story, so the story really came quite easily. My other significant piece of preparation was reading Colin Turnbull's *The Forest People*, about the BaMbuti of the Ituri forest. I've stuck with his spellings and explanations throughout so please blame him (via a necromancer, as he has passed on) if there is anything wrong with the facts. Also, before anyone tells me that N'geeso is actually Wochua and not Mbuti, I have an answer- Kimagi could have married into the Mbuti.

While I do love these adventure stories from the 1920s, they often have elements that are potentially problematic for today's reader and writer—like the thinly-veiled analogy for colonialism of the Congo. As a writer from a former colony, I can't just let this slide—so I introduced Mpumelelo Matthias, a sort of mouthpiece for my post-colonial angst. Having said that, he is very much not just a token character. For this story, much more than the last few stories I've written, I plotted the story well in advance. This really helped with the flow when writing it, but of course I had to leave a bit of room for the characters who sometimes did other things.

**TERRY WIJESURIYA** - a is a student of history, who seems to spend her whole life writing in different forms. She reads not wisely nor too well, but certainly widely. She is inspired by whatever book she read last, but has a special soft spot in her heart for Orientalist swashbucklers like *Lost Horizon*. In her spare time she runs a sporadic fan blog for J.T. Edson's floating outfit series (theysabelkid.wordpress.com). Her dream is to be a chain-smoking, hard-drinking pulp fiction author, which would be more likely to come true if she wasn't a teetotaler who never smokes.

# JUNGLE CALLS

### By Bob Madison

**O**utside my window was the jungle.

A tangled mass of green, thick and overgrown beyond human imagination. As the bright red slivers sunset played over the treetops, I could sense the forest teeming with life. Waves of heat floated towards me, and I staggered backward at the stench.

The jungle always stinks. Rotted vegetation, mud and damp, and the thick, savage smell of animals. As if to underscore my thoughts, a piercing cry penetrated the trees. It came loud and shrill, and quickly cut short on a strangled note.

The jungle had claimed another victim.

I let the gauzy material of the curtain fall and turned back to my room. Overhead, a ceiling fan spun lazily. The cane-backed chairs would not be out of place in the poshest of gentlemen's clubs, and the walls were lined with books now mildewed by the damp.

This is my home. I haven't always lived in this godforsaken hell, and I was once a different man. But that was years ago. Too long ago to remember.

I took the crystal decanter from the bar and poured another brandy. I added flat soda from the siphon just before the polite knock at the door.

"Come."

Kunwhald, my house boy. Like all Watusi, incredibly tall, and the top of his head brushes against the door frame. Small, brilliantly white finger bones hang from each ear. He stands tall, as always, proud and capable.

"Yes?"

"Visitor. Says she must see you." His voice is like controlled thunder.

"A visitor? Here?"

"Come with guide and two bearers. Says she walk many days. You want I should send her away?"

I considered. "No. Send her in."

I straightened my white jacket and ran a hand through my hair. There was another knock and Kunwhald opened the door and bowed. She followed close behind him.

She was tall and her blond hair was lank from too long without a washing. Sensibly, she had gone without make-up during her expedition, but the effect was still worthwhile. Eyes of rich blue stared from under her pith helmet and her lips pouted at me. The vision of holding her in my arms and pressing my lips against hers floated somewhere in the back of my mind, and I smiled at it.

"Kane?" she asked. "Richmond Kane?"

I nodded. "Brandy and soda?"

"Thanks." She came close to me as I poured. She took the drink with a smile and managed a healthy gulp. "You're not an easy man to find."

"I know."

"The last word I had was in Burma. You were flying a Graumann Goose and had taken some nuns to a leper colony. You were the only pilot who'd do it. Before that, you were in Africa, tracking elephants for the Natural History Museum with Akeley. Nobody's heard of you since."

"What ever happened to Akeley?"

"Skull crushed. Elephant. Died in the bush."

I finished my drink. "Tough break."

"A lot has happened in the real world," she told me.

"Yeah?"

"Roosevelt is president, and he's offering the country a new deal. Pictures talk. A man in Italy says he's going to make the trains run on time."

"Imagine that."

"You going to offer me a seat?"

"What do you want?"

"Thanks," she said, sitting in one of the wicker chairs. She ran the damp glass across her forehead. "This story won't take long. I've come here, Mr. Kane, to ask for your help."

I took a pull on my drink. "Me?"

"Yes. The Boga tribe. I see from your reaction that you remember them."

I felt my body grow cold. "Vividly."

"The story has it that they are about a hundred miles south of here. No one knows for sure, or if they do, they're not saying. Of course," she sipped her drink, "I've heard that you've been there."

I said nothing.

"Legend says that there are two idols that they worship, more like totem poles than statues. And both of them are made of solid gold. Or so I've heard it said."

I stood. Two more seconds and I would show her the door.

"I financed one expedition to find the Bogas and buy the idols. At a price, of course."

"Of course."

"It hasn't returned. Three white men, including the expedition leader, and nine native bearers. Vanished without a trace. Mr. Kane, the expedition leader was my husband and business partner, and, I want him back."

"What makes you think I'd help you?"

"You have that reputation."

"That's all in the past. I don't help anyone anymore. It hurts too much. And even if I were to do something for somebody, I wouldn't go near the Bogas. You have no idea of what you're asking and maybe it's for the best that you don't." My mind flooded with memories: swirling bodies in the night, the bonfires, the screams of agony. My knees weakened, but if I didn't go on, I feared I'd pass out. "My trip to Boga country wasn't entirely successful."

"What happened there?"

"I was captured and kept prisoner. They ... did things to me."

I went to the door and quietly opened it.

She smiled at me. "Fifteen thousand dollars."

"No."

"Twenty-five thousand dollars."

"Look, Miss, I've made more than enough money for both the necessities and luxuries of life. This discussion has ended. Nothing you can say would convince me to take you there."

Now she stood. "The expedition leader, and my husband, was your brother, David Kane. How do you do? I'm Jean Kane, your sister-in-law."

Two nights later, I twisted in bed, unable to sleep.

My bedroom was thick with the sickly sweet jungle smell and my sweat drenched the bedclothes. I clawed at the mosquito net overhead, my body racked with the memory of torture. In the black pit of my unconscious, I could hear the jungle drums. Their insistent beat pounded my temples until I thought I would scream. The vision of hands, dreadful claws at the end of impossibly long arms, came to me. Arms reaching out.

Focus, I told myself. Focus on the job at hand.

David Kane, my brother. I haven't seen him in eighteen years. He was the youngest of we four sons, and the only brother I spoke to after we had all grown up. We drifted apart as our lives went in separate directions, but he's still my brother and I love him.

Jean had caught me up as best she could. She and David met and married a few years ago, just outside of Johannesburg. He had been working on a degree in anthropology; she was the daughter of a failed diamond miner. It was from her father that she learned of the golden idols, and she and David planned an expedition.

And now, he's in Boga country.

Savage faces came to me in the darkness. Teeth filed to sharp points, mad brown eyes flashing in faces smeared with blood...

I climbed out of bed and toweled off. Slipping into a dressing gown, I stepped downstairs into the library for a drink. The siphon spat soda into my brandy and I shivered before I drank.

I heard a sound and turned. Jean sat in the darkness near the corner window. She wore a pale, almost transparent nightgown, a glass in her hand.

"Couldn't sleep either?"

"I was thinking of out there," she said, pointing to the window with her glass. "It's another world. Trees and vegetation run riot, the whole world like it was over one million years ago. It's the prehistoric age of tooth and claw, right outside your window. Animal law, the law of the jungle, is the only rule, and the weak find themselves dead."

I sat on the floor, close to her chair. I could smell the scent of her body. "What made him go? It's madness."

"First, he was just curious. Science and all of that. Meaningless. Then we started thinking of the gold. Imagine, twin idols, reaching into the sky, made of solid gold. A fortune, ripe for the taking."

"It's not yours."

"It could be. My father spent his entire life hunting for diamonds. He never found any. Have you ever been poor, Mr. Kane? Dirt-eating poor?"

"Yes." That memory hurt, too.

"Then you know. I've been hungry. I've been in rags. I've done things for money that were wrong, that I shouldn't have. I did things with men, just so my father and I could eat. I told all of this to David and I think part of him ached for me. He went out there, into the jungle, because of my pain. He went out there, to bring back to life the part of me that died when I was poor."

I said nothing.

She turned to the window. Her voice lost all inflection. "I don't have character. I don't pretend I do. So, I let him go. My need was greater."

"And are you going out there to find him, or the idols?"

The door opened slowly, and the sleek barrel of an elephant gun snaked into the room.

Behind me, Jean gasped. I slowly rose.

The door opened completely and Kunwhald stood in the frame. "I thought I heard voices."

"Just us," I said.

"We leave at sun-up," he said, lowering the gun.

"Yeah. I'm just on my way back to bed. Jean, you had better hit the hay, too."

"I think I'll sit here just a few minutes more. Thanks."

"Goodnight," I mumbled as Kunwhald followed me out the door. On the stairs I said: "Keep an eye on her."

It was like a holiday in hell.

The bright red sun started to creep over the forest, the sky filled with the color of blood. Kunwhald had gotten six native bearers from a neighboring village. He led the way into the bush while I brought up the rear. Jean stayed close to me.

The bearers held additional guns and ammunition, along with food, water, and the makings of camp. They looked at the jungle ahead with grim faces. What were they thinking, I wondered? And what did they knew, or intuit, that was a mystery to me?

My rifle felt good in my hand and I held it at the ready. It was 7.9 mm. German Mauser — a good gun for the bush. Jean carried a silver plated automatic I had given her and it hung from a holster strapped to her thin waist. Kunwhald, ever distrustful of the trappings of my world, pressed forward with nothing more than a loincloth and spear.

*a closed canopy over-head blotted out the sun.*

We had not marched long before the trees surrounding my home grew thicker. Soon Kunwhald stopped, standing at the very edge of the bush. He turned and looked at me. I nodded him on.

We stepped into the jungle, a twilight world of impenetrable forest. The trees clustered thickly, creating a closed canopy over-head that blotted out the sun. It was another world, one that had neither sympathy nor patience for the puny animal that was man. A mad tangle of vines clutched at my feet and I pulled myself free with each angry step.

Sounds, too, were different. Cries of victory and anguish could be heard in the far-off corners of the forest, as if we were being watched by a crowd of savage animals invisible to us. The howls were hollow and distant, making me sick at soul.

I choked on the jungle smell — the thick aroma of vegetation, damp, and rot. Up ahead, Kunwhald had already unsheathed a machete and had started to hack our way through the tangle.

"What about the Bogas?" Jean interrupted my reverie. It was like a slap into wakefulness.

"What about them?"

"The idols. Were they there? Could you see the gold?" Her voiced was a hushed whisper.

"Does it matter, now?"

She stared ahead, into the jungle. "It could."

"And David?"

"Of course he matters!" she snapped.

"They are twin idols, both about twenty-five feet tall. They're a series of heads, one on top of another, representing their gods. Where the gold came from, no one knows. Who built them is a mystery. Surely the kind of work I saw was completely beyond the Bogas. Both idols have tremendous significance in the Boga's religion."

"Which is what?"

"Boga mysticism is a mystery to me. And if it has any bearing on the way they live their lives, I don't want to know about it."

"Your scars are deep."

"And not just physical. It was madness to take you along, madness to drag you into this."

"He's my husband! And I dragged you."

I kept walking, each footstep settling into the soft earth of the jungle. "He's probably dead."

"You got out alive."

"Barely."

"But you did."

"If we get out of Boga country, you'll have seen things that you'll keep for the rest of your life. Are you still ready to go in, knowing that?"

Finally she faced me. "What would your answer be?"

I said nothing.

We stopped only intermittently, when the heat and the damp and the smell were too much for us. My joints ached at the exertion and my heart grew heavy. We set up camp at sunset. By Kunwhald's calculations, we have traveled ten miles.

We built a poor fire; damp wood and sodden earth fought us. Kunwhald and I took turns standing watch; Jean wanted a turn, but I insisted she sleep. She would need it.

We broke camp at dawn and pressed on. After a couple of hours, the ground began to get softer and to tilt downward.

"Damn."

"What is it?" she asked.

"We're hitting swampland."

"That bad?"

"Dangerous. Very dangerous."

Soon the earth was nothing more than black soup. Kunwhald kept up ahead, maintaining his balance while holding his spear high overhead. The bearers struggled beneath their loads, often sliding beneath the cases they carried.

"Water!" Kunwhald cried.

And there it was, finally, the swamp. It was little more than a field of dark, fetid water. I shuffled beyond the bearers and stood beside Kunwhald. The water stretched out as far as the eye could see, both straight ahead and east-west.

"Go around it?" I asked.

"Don't know how far around. Could set us back too long," he said.

"The rainy season was months ago."

"Should be shallow. Walk through it?"

"Don't have much of a choice." I motioned to the men and they lifted their packs with trepidation.

Jean came up behind me. "What's the matter?"

"We have to go through the swamp."

"So?"

"They're afraid. Don't blame them. Quicksands, leeches, God knows what."

"Damn them!" She pushed her loose fitting pants into her tall boots and stepped into the water.

Kunwhald shot me a look, then followed. He made his way behind her, his tread deliberate.

I stepped in, my feet sinking into the soft mud. The water swelled over my ankles, bits of earth fluttering in the water. My boots held tight and my feet stayed dry.

Jean pushed on recklessly, the water at the mid-point of her shins. Some of the trees had rotted at their roots and now lay partially buried in the muck. She pushed her way through them, Kunwhald close behind.

I motioned for the bearers to follow, and they did, howling as they stepped into the wet. My nerves ran through me like fire, my senses heightened to the constant danger. Something roiled under the water inches away from my boot, then swam away.

Snakes. And the bearers were bare-legged. My grip tightened on my rifle and I paused so the men could catch up to me.

After twenty minutes, we had gotten halfway through, with drier land hovering in the distance.

A few feet more and the water grew shallow. Jean and Kunwhald navigated past a withered hulk of tree, with me following. I felt the ground start to rise up underfoot when I heard the scream.

I twisted, rifle at the ready. One of the bearers had stiffened in agony, dropping his case containing our tents into the swamp. He screamed and tugged at his leg, the withered log I had passed grabbing his ankle.

I splashed over, brandishing my Mauser. I could hear Kunwhald behind me, racing through the muck.

The warty and knotted log twisted with a horrible life of its own. It writhed beneath the slimy surface of the water, muscles coiling under its reptilian skin. The log was really a small croc, and it had the man by the leg. I lowered the tip my Mauser into the water and fired.

There was a tremendous explosion, throwing up water and blood like a geyser. The recoil knocked me back and I staggered backwards, struggling to keep balance. There was a thrashing underfoot and the croc was gone. The man jabbered and lurched towards me, collapsing in my arms.

Kunwhald and I helped him out and put him to rest on the damp ground around the swamp. With an ear-splitting shriek, he started to wail and pray.

The wound wasn't bad ... from the space between the teeth, it was a little croc of no more than nine or eleven feet. The bite seemed to go as deep as the bone and it bled freely. But there was no ripping of the flesh and he could move the foot without too much pain. Some disinfectant and a bandage and he would be fine.

"Can he walk?" Jean asked.

"Think so, but he won't be carrying anything for a while."

Kunwhald had stepped back into the swamp, spear held high and ready to attack. With his free hand, he pulled the tent case from the muck.

"It'll be heavier," he said. "Wet. Damage?"

"None, except the Mauser," I said. I held the rifle up for inspection. There was a bulge in the barrel where it had hit the water. The pressure pushed it out and the gun was virtually useless.

"Good metal in these Mausers. Foolish of me to stick it into the water. A different gun, it would've exploded and killed a couple of us. As it is, I may have killed us all."

Jean spoke. "How?"

"Fire a gun here and everything within miles knows where you are. Sending up a flare would've been just as effective."

"You mean?"

"I mean, the Bogas may find us before we find them."

One of the bearers had guns strapped to him and I pulled a .256 Mannlicher short barrel from his back. I pushed Kunwhald and the men on and brought up the rear. Progress was hampered by our man's injured ankle, but still we made good time for the bush. At day's end, Kunwhald had estimated a progression of eight miles.

Night fell quickly in the eternal twilight of the jungle. Cutting from the higher branches we found enough dry wood for a fire. The tents were damp and built close to the fire to fight any mildew. I've seen heavy canvas rot through in just a few days.

I sat by the fire, sipping from a silver flask. I had Kunwhald double the guard and the men stood just within the range of the firelight, guns ready.

Jean came out of her tent. She was drawn close to the fire. I could see the flame flicker in her eyes. "Anything?"

"Not yet." I looked into the blackness. "I've got a feeling."

She looked out into the blackness. Silence answered her.

I sat by the fire until well after midnight. My body ached at the thought of tomorrow's trek. With that in mind, I rotated the guards and turned in. The thick smell of the swamp had eaten into the canvas of the tent. Two cots were readied and Kunwhald lie on his back in a loincloth, his eyes open.

I bade him goodnight and crawled into my cot. He said nothing and when I lowered the lamp, I saw that his eyes were still open.

It happened quickly.

The screaming woke me. Kunwhald was up in a flash, his hard, lean body reaching for his spear. I tumbled out of bed, reaching for my Mannlicher. With a rip, someone had cut through our tent wall. In the gloom came the flash of a knife. Kunwhald reared back with his spear, but my Mannlicher exploded, throwing the invader back through the tent.

"Get to the girl," I barked. "I'll keep them back!"

He followed me through the cut opening and we backed around the tent. The situation was clear in a glance. The campfire illuminated the corpses of our guards, their bodies pierced with the long spears favored by the Bogas. The few bearers that remained were struggling hand-to-hand with the Bogas.

No sign of Jean.

Kunwhald, spear held high, dashed to her tent. A Boga from the bush trailed him, stone knife in hand. I cut him down with my Mannlicher before he got too close. The flash from the barrel was blinding, the retort like thunder in the damp air.

My bearer with the injured foot grappled in the dirt, he and a Boga twisting in circles. I couldn't get a clear shot and raced to his side. The butt end of my rifle put the Boga out and I helped the bearer to his feet.

He smiled a quick thanks before his face contorted in agony. I heard the horrible wet sound of pierced flesh and looked down at the spear tip that had come through his chest. With a gurgle the bearer fell to his knees, then his face. The spear stood out of his back like an exclamation point.

With the bearer down, the Boga that got him now stood directly in my line of fire. He reached to the ground for another spear and I blew his chest away with my Mannlicher.

More screams. I scrambled, Mannlicher at the ready. Kunwhald stumbled backward out of Jean's tent. He jabbed at two knife-wielding Bogas with his spear. One of them lunged and Kunwhald swiped him with the tip, ripping a gash in the man's naked torso. With a jerk, he brought the blunt bottom of the spear to the man's jaw, knocking him back and out.

Still no sign of Jean.

A spear sailed past my head. I felt the rush of air and the faintest brush of the wood as it sped past my cheek. Another inch and it would've buried itself in my brain. The Boga who tried for me started backing away into the bush.

With a savage smile, I raised my Mannlicher, ready to cancel him out.

Then, a fierce blow to the back of my head, and all was blackness.

*Beside me I could make out the figures of Kunwhald and Jean.*

The first thing I knew was the pounding in my head.

I tried to open my eyes, then closed them in pain. A wave of nausea passed through me, and I swallowed it back.

Next I became conscious of the intense heat. My body was drenched with sweat and my clothes had clung to me. My cheeks and forehead were smothered in hot air.

Blearily, I managed to open my eyes. I was in a darkened room of compacted straw, a hut of some kind. A dim, red glow from an overhanging oil lamp provided the room with faint light. Beside me I could make out the figures of Kunwhald and Jean. Both of them were bound, ankles together, hands behind their backs.

I moved towards them, only to realize that I too was bound. Waves of pain sped through my body as I tried to move and I stopped, exhausted. I wriggled my fingers, now trapped behind me, praying the blood would start to circulate again.

I realized that the banging in my head was actually the sound of drums in the distance. I groaned inwardly and started to sweat again. The blow to my head must have caused a concussion. Everything around me, I thought, could just be a horrible delusion, the hallucination of a man with a heady injury. I blinked such thoughts away, for down that road lie madness.

My body quivered in horrible anticipation. Every torture the Bogas had inflicted on me returned in phantom torments, my body squirming in imagined agony. Once again I felt their hot spears bury themselves in my knees, the skin peeled from my back...

Kunwhald woke first. He managed to sit upright, quickly taking stock of the situation. His face grim, he nudged Jean. She twitched with a moan, her body resisting consciousness.

"How long you been awake?" he asked.

"Not long. The drums, do you hear them?"

He grunted.

"Who'll be first, I wonder?"

He looked into the blackness, saying nothing.

I swallowed hard. "We could kill her. Now, ourselves. Before they get to her."

"Have to decide soon."

I looked at her. In the red gloom, she was almost supernaturally lovely. Her blond hair reflected the light like flame and her sleeping face was that of an angel. Her chest fluttered. Soon she would awake.

"Not yet. It's too soon," I said.

And the drums stopped.

My heart filled with terror as I looked at Jean. As if on que, her eyes blinked open. They filled with pain as she struggled against her bonds, making little mewling sounds.

"Don't," I said. "It'll only make them tighter. It's cat gut. Leopard, usually. It'll cut into your skin deeper than you can imagine, and before you know it, you bleed to death."

"Bastards," she muttered.

"Quiet. The drums have stopped and I know what's next. They'll take one of us."

Her mouth worked, choking back a gasp. "What'll they do?"

I didn't answer. "Kunwhald, you can talk to Boga lingo?"

He nodded.

"Talk to them, tell them everything. Tell them my brother was lost, and we were looking for him. Tell them—"

Jean's face contorted with a sick look, and she started to crawl back. I turned and saw a shadow at the hut opening.

"Damn."

It came closer, a figure shrouded in night, coming bigger and bigger. It filled the doorway, then stepped into the light.

A Boga. My blood turned cold at the sight of him. He looked like his fellow tribesmen: small ears purposely boxed to cauliflower, teeth filed down to points, and the blank, blood lusting-stare of a psychopath. His head was shaved and the thick, knotty tribal scar ran across his pate to the back of his neck. Dressed in skins, he looked like some great, prehistoric beast.

"Tell him, Kunwhald."

Kunwhald started to speak and I could hear a gargled version of David's name. The Boga held up his palm and Kunwhald went silent.

The Boga looked at us, clinically.

"Try not to be afraid," I said. "It's fear that they want. They suck it out of you and grow fat on it."

The scrutiny lasted only a second more. Then, two more Bogas, shorter and squatter than the first but both with the filed teeth, shaved heads and scars, joined him. Without a word, he pointed at Kunwhald.

They came, hauling him up by the shoulders. I tried to get to my knees and was pushed back with a bare foot to my chest. Jean rolled away, pressing her body against the straw wall.

Kunwhald rose. A Boga cut away the bounds of his ankles with a stone knife, then used the point at his back to guide him out. He threw me a look and was taken away.

"Bastards!" I screamed. "Bring him back! Leave him alone!"

Kunwhald was gone and the tall Boga stood at the door, smiling at me. Then, turning, he left.

There was silence. Then Jean spoke. "Will they kill him?"

"Not right away. Not all at once."

She started towards me, slithering across the floor like a snake. "We're getting out of here."

"Just like that?"

"Just like that."

It took her a few minutes, but she dragged herself to me. We sat back to back, stiffened fingers working on the fine wire. I clawed at her bonds, pinching her skin. She struggled with mine, her longer nails scratching at me. Soon, I felt a warm wetness flood my palm, and I knew the cat gut had dug into my wrists, drawing blood.

"It's not working," she said.

"Dammit, stay still. I can't get hold of anything."

"Wait a minute." Grunting, she twisted and flopped on her belly behind me. I felt her hair brush against the back of my arms and her warm breath on my hands. Her face pressed to my wrists, she started biting at the rope. Her teeth pinched my skin and I could feel her tongue churning as she licked and softened the bond. Her incisors grabbed and worked on a strand, let go, and started again. I felt the gut cut tighter as she pulled and the blood started to flow again.

Finally, she worked a strand loose, and reared back with her head, pulling it along with her teeth. Another stand came loose and soon the gut started to unravel.

It took a few minutes more, as she bit and pulled like a jungle cat. Soon, I was able to wrench one had free. An agonizing sting worked through my wrists and I examined them in the gloom. They bled freely, but I don't think fatally.

I turned to Jean. Her mouth was smeared with my blood and she slumped on the floor, exhausted. I rolled her on her stomach and removed my belt, using the sharp edge of the buckle to cut the gut that held her. The gut left thin, blood-red lines, but no real damage. Next I did her feet and then my own.

I ripped the pockets out of the insides of my pants and bandaged my wrists, tying the knot of each with my free hand and my teeth. A red stain spotted instantly, but the flow had stopped.

I rose unsteadily to my feet. I lifted Jean up, her body shaking.

"Tear away some of the hut wall," she said. "We can escape through the back."

"First David. And Kunwhald."

"Kunwhald is dead."

"There's still hope. And David."

"David's not here," she said, sick. "He never was."

It hit me with a jolt. "What?"

"He was never here. You've been to Boga country, you saw the idols. You were the only one I could use." She lurched towards the wall. "I had to say something, anything to make you come."

I came at her. "You *lied* to me."

"The idols," she murmured blankly. "The idols."

I spun her around by the shoulders, my fingers burying themselves in her flesh. "You brought us here for the idols." I could barely speak, and in my rage my breath came in snorts. White sheets of lightning flashed before my eyes and I felt some essential part of me unhinge and float away. "You brought us here for nothing," my words gasped through clenched teeth. I could feel my hands come closer together and before I knew it, I had her by the throat. I squeezed, my hands and face growing hot.

She gagged and clawed at my hands, pulling up clumps of my flesh. Still I squeezed, my muscles tensing as I choked the life out of her. Her thick tongue thrust between her lips and her eyes glassed over.

Suddenly, the horror of what I was doing hit me, and I let go. She dropped to the floor, gasping. "You evil bitch. I should feed you to the Bogas."

She cried and choked, struggling with air and her emotions. "I had to come. I had to. You don't understand. Nothing. I had nothing."

I left her there, pacing the hut. Torn by fury and terror, I stumbled about for something to do. I knew that if I turned my attentions to Jean, I could all too easily kill her. *Channel the rage*, I thought. *Make it work for you.* My heart hammered in my chest, my temples continued to pound.

"I had to have you with me," her voice was a harsh whisper.

I continued to pace.

"It wasn't hard to discover things about you. A few questions, an afternoon with some old newspapers and I had what I needed." She started to massage her throat. "David is unharmed. I've never even met him."

I stood over her, my hands balled to fists.

"The things I told you, about my past, were true." She looked away from me, her voice distant. "I heard tell of the idols from one of the men I knew in Cape Town. It was like a promise of heaven. Gods of gold, just what I needed to save my soul."

And then, just as suddenly as they stopped, the drums started once more.

"Kunwhald," I whispered.

She looked at me, pleading.

"If he's dead, expect no mercy from me. You can count on it."

I looked around the hut, the earthen floor barren except for a few strands of straw. And my belt, dropped when I had cut us free.

"On the floor," I said. "Hands behind your back, feet together. Play dead, if you can."

"What are you going to do?"

"The same. I'll jump them if I have to. If I can get my belt around one of their throats, I could use him as a shield."

I fell to the floor, holding my hands behind my back. I could see huddled figures in the shadows outside, lugging something with them.

The figures stepped in and I repressed an impulse to run foreword as I saw they carried Kunwhald. They threw him to the floor, leered at me, and made for the flaps of the tent. I watched them go into the blackness and the blackness swallowed them.

I dashed to his side in an instant. Jean hovered behind me.

Kunwhald had gotten off easy. The tips of each of his fingers had been split, the flesh seared where hot needles were thrust into the nerve ends. The nails of each finger had been peeled away, raw, red patches where they once had been.

A quick examination told me the joints of his toes had been broken, and the skin at the bottom of his feet ripped away.

"Jesus," she moaned.

"This is just the start. If they get you, by the time they're finished you'll wish that I had killed you."

"Can he walk?"

"Don't know." I ripped strips from my bush jacket, bundling his raw feet. Waking would be an agony for him, but there was little choice. I slapped him several times and his eyelids fluttered before he snapped into instant consciousness. He remained stoic and courageous, like all of his tribe, but I could read the pain in his face.

"Hundreds," he said. "Hundreds of them. Great wickedness. Ritual, awful."

"Kunwhald, we have to make a break for it. Is there anything you saw, anything that could help?"

He looked into space like a man drunk. He battled memories of the past hour, sifting through them.

"Guns," he said. "Makings of camp kept in great pile."

"The idols," Jean asked. "Did you see the idols?"

Outside, the drums continued.

Kunwhald lapsed back into unconsciousness.

"Keep an eye on him," I told Jean. "I'm going to cut my way through the rear end of the hut. Wait for me. If you hear them coming, break away through the back and head for the bush. You won't get far, but at least try."

"What about him?"

"Take care of yourself. You seem to be good at that."

I went to the opposite wall and started tearing away huge clumps of straw. There was always the chance that guards were posted outside the hut, but I

*"Take care of yourself. You seem to be good at that."*

hoped they thought we were too tightly tied to escape. At least, that was my hope. The straw quickly thinned as I clawed my way through. A black gaping hole waited me. Before setting off, I took one more look at the hut. Kunwhald, sprawled on the floor, remained unconscious. Jean stood over him, her eyes boring into me.

I bent my head and stepped into the void.

The night air stank of sweat, bonfire, and jungle. I darted around, struggling to remain steady on my legs. I cautiously circled the hut. A Boga stood there, stone knife tucked into the waistband of the skins he wore. He bald head seemed to glow in the dark, the purple-black scar like a huge vein. He stood, looking into the bush, transported by the sound of drums.

The hut stood off, away from the village. It was on the other end of a slight rise and I could see the brilliant red and yellow flame of their campfire. A shower of sparks flew up towards heaven.

To my surprise, I found I still had my belt wrapped around my right hand. Opening it to its full length, I crept up on my man. I snared him around the neck and twisted with everything I had. His arms flailed, and I think he reached for his knife, but his hands began to twitch convulsively. In minutes it was over. I dragged the body into the bush and took his knife. Like any jungle predator, I now had a fang.

I crept to the edge of the bush, using the great trees as cover. Faceless things scurried in the dark forest floor, but I continued on. Their village came into focus, the bonfire lighting it with a hellish brilliance.

Every detail was seared into my memory the last time I was here. It hadn't changed. A huge bonfire blazed like the pits of hell itself. The Bogas danced a circle around it, their bodies glistening with sweat. Some of them tore the animal skins they wore from their bodies and threw them into the inferno, screaming curses. The conflagration threw a terrible glow on their faces, firelight dancing in their eyes like bits of lightning.

Seated high in a simple sedan chair of jungle wood sat the High Priest. He looked down on the worshippers with a twisted smile, his filed-down fangs pressing into his bottom lip. Beside him, a simple earthen bowl with raw meat.

My eyes trailed the blaze of the fire, following its sweep with the jungle breeze. My eyes grew accustomed to the glare, and I could now see the idols beyond.

Again, I looked in wonder at their golden gods. They stood upon a large stone altar and both spires reached thirty feet into the night. The gold glinted in the fire light and stood like twin, blinding streaks of lightning. The image burned into my retina, and closing my eyes, I could see it still.

Graven images were carved into them, monstrous, misshapen heads. Many sported fangs like those the Bogas imitated, with eyes buried in shadowy hollows. Others were fashioned like the withered, decomposed faces of men long dead. Angry, bestial faces, evil human faces with animal horns or goat-like snouts glared down at the flame with golden eyes. A blasphemous mixture of man and ape, golden mouth open in a silent roar, topped one of the totem poles. A tentacled, one-eyed thing topped the other, like a madman's version of an octopus. The poles, like the stone altar, were festooned with obscure hieroglyphs.

I stood, transfixed with awe at the sight. Never had I seen relics both so hallowed and so repellent. Little wonder the Bogas worshipped them. They were a wonderful, dreadful achievement — the enduring monument of a lost and twisted people.

In the distance were the simple huts they lived in. Near a group of supply huts lay heaped the stores of our expedition. The boxes, many of the broken, had been raided, and the contents strewn on the damp jungle floor. Firelight flickered on the barrel of my Mannlicher.

The goods were unguarded and the Bogas remained focused on the fire and the steady rhythm of the drum. I continued through the darkened jungle rim, sneaking around the village. My progress was slow as the bush shredded my clothes and tore at my skin. The night about me was thick with mosquitoes and the damp air smelled foul and sick.

I could not keep track of time, but it seemed an eternity before I reached the stores. Peering from behind the bush, I made certain I was unobserved and crept to the stash. The Bogas still danced around the bonfire, which threw up smoke into the black, black night like a factory. I hit it at a crouch, and my hands closed gratefully around my Mannlicher. I smiled.

Then, just as I had it in my hands, the drums stopped.

My heart stopped dead. I fell to my knees, hiding behind the pile of boxes. I grabbed an ammunition pouch. To my surprise, underneath it was Jean's nickel plated automatic. I stuffed that in my pocket, too.

With the drums gone silent, I knew they'd be back at our prison. I dashed back into the bush and tore recklessly through the forest. The Bogas moved with a slow, stately progression, and I made good time. I reached the hut before them, and scampering around, entered through the hole I had torn in the back.

I was later than I thought. As I scrambled in, the tall Boga from before entered the tent. Jean stood in my way, but still his powerful form loomed around her.

"Duck!"

She hit the dirt in an instant and my Mannlicher spit a torrent of death. The Boga somersaulted over backwards and landed with a sick thud. The ground grew wet with blood.

I pulled Jean up by the shoulder and pressed the automatic into her hand. "Help me with him!" I barked, hauling Kunwhald up the by shoulder. He was dazed, his face looking into mine blankly. She held him as I crouched over and draped him over my left shoulder. The weight was tremendous and my sore body screamed in protest.

We lunged for the door, right into a nest of Bogas.

About twenty of them, standing right in front of the entrance. The fire in the background played over the tops of their bald heads and their scars seemed to pulse like giant veins. It was so silent, I could hear my heart beat. A smaller Boga stood closest and with a savage cry lifted his spear.

Jean's automatic replied with a deafening thunder.

The spear went wild as the man fell. My right arm brought up the Mannlicher and I fired into the crowd. Jean spotted two of them before I could fire again. They ran, screaming into the night.

"The bush?" she asked.

"Into camp!" I ran, hefting Kunwhald on my shoulder. I knew if I could do as much damage as possible, we might hold them off long enough to put some distance between us.

Confusion galloped through the village. Bogas bumbled around, uncertain whether to head for the prison hut or run to their homes. Some kowtowed before the High Priest, who stood on his sedan chair and gazed into the night. I hefted the Mannlicher and fired, the flash from the rifle streaking like lightning. He crumpled in a heap and dropped into the crowd. The Bogas howled and fell on him like carrion birds.

We ran openly through them, the roar of the fire drowning out the screams. Some of the more courageous bulls mulled together, gathering spears. Jean fired a volley into them while running, dropping many. My Mannlicher finished the argument.

"We're going to make it!" I heard her say right before she stopped dead.

I almost tumbled into her. "What?"

She pointed. I followed her gaze up. The idols continued to glow brilliantly in the firelight. The evil faces flickered with a blasphemous life of their own.

"The idols," she said, and ran towards them.

"Jean!" I took a half step after her and stopped. I debated following her for a handful of seconds, turned, and carried Kunwhald into the jungle.

I made good time despite the extra weight. I sped through the village and jumped into the jungle. I pushed my way through, the ground moving upward on a slight incline. I knew the Bogas would soon be behind me. For all my speed, my mind was blank except for a sense of sick despair. I knew in my heart of hearts that we would not make it.

The gunshots stopped me. It could only be Jean. I stopped, lungs afire, and lowered Kunwhald to the ground. Bracing myself, I turned back for another look.

The Boga village was spread like a great diorama beneath me. Jean had just picked off a Boga that had gotten too close. She blew smoke from the muzzle of her automatic and concentrated on the idols. Using the butt end of her automatic, she pounded at the gold of the ape-headed one.

I heard a high pitched wailing sound. The wind rose and swirled in circular currents. The fire blew in the frenzied gusts of air, sparks flying. Bogas all over the village stopped mid-step, and started twisting and singing. The wailing grew louder and the fire roared.

Jean continued the hack away, the wind whipping her blond hair.

"Jean!" I called, but there was nothing I could do. She was too far away, the noise too great. I could only sit and watch.

The idols started to tremble; the gold grew paler despite the fury of the flames. Then both started to expand slightly, like huge animals taking a deep breath. A savage roar, like that of a prehistoric animal, boomed from out of nowhere.

Jean stopped, stepping back. Her gaze trailed up the idol and she screamed.

On top, the hideous human-ape face began to move. Browns knitted and the eyes came alive with a malefic frenzy. Saliva like molten gold dripped from the razor-sharp teeth. It roared again.

The length of the golden body started to vibrate, all of the heads coming to life. The corpse-like faces sputtered and spat green bile, the savage beast-men worked their dreadful mouths as their eyes lit. They gibbered and growled with unearthly voices. The pole sprouted arms, as if from nowhere, golden arms incredibly long, with sharp pointed fingers.

Behind her, the octopus on the other idol began to writhe. The tentacles slipped down the length of its many headed body, leaving a dripping trail of golden slime. They glistened in the firelight, coiling like snakes. The single eye of the thing blinked, looking down at Jean.

She had her automatic in seconds. In one fluid motion she took aim and fired up into the ape face. But it kept coming at her. She spat three more bullets, backing away, closer to the other idol. It was only when she stepped into its twisting tentacles that terror overcame her. She threw her automatic at the ape, crouching to run.

Too late. The long arms of the ape-like idol had her by the shoulders and lifted her effortlessly. She screamed, her arms and legs flailing madly. She tore and scratched at the thing as it bore her closer to its mouth.

The tentacles from the other idol reached out, wrapping around one ankle, then the other. Both held her suspended between them, and even in the distance I could hear her screams. Another tentacle wound around her waist, pulling her closer. One of the lower heads cackled, golden fangs afire.

The Bogas circled the base, chanting and dancing like a people possessed. Some dropped to the ground in supplication, rolling in mud and religious mania.

The ape thing brought her closer to its mouth, the drool now spilling down the side of its body in rivers. It's long, golden tongue snaked out of its mouth and tickled the side of her head. She thrashed, both of them pulling her in opposite directions. Her screams were unbearable and I felt my insides grow cold.

The ape-thing tugged her closer and sank its fangs into her shoulder. She convulsed and twitched, then went limp like a rag doll. It was still biting at her when the tentacles snatched her away. It slid her up the length of its pole, its coils wrapping her securely. Consciousness hit her again as she was lifted her up. Its eye glared at her.

I drew up my Mannlicher and took aim. The distance was bad and the wind against me, but I've taken more difficult shots and scored. With luck I could do a body shot that would put her out.

Kunwhald grabbed my arm, wrenching the gun from my grasp. "No," he said. "Bogas hear. They follow."

It was only for a second that I thought about it. Then I took Kunwhald by the shoulder and helped him up. Silently, we crept into the jungle.

**THE END**

# ABOUT JUNGLE CALLS

Ever since I was a kid, I've been obsessed with jungles. I was lucky enough to grow up during the "Nostalgia Craze" of the 70s, so tons of 30s-40s pop culture funneled its way through my young and over-excited brain.

Two key pieces of that were, of course, *King Kong* and *The Most Dangerous Game*. Then I started reading Edgar Rice Burroughs' *Tarzan* novels and soon the whole notion of "going into the bush" obsessed me. All I thought about was traveling to the wild parts of the earth, and I spent a lot of time reading about Sir Richard Burton, Frank Buck, Trader Horn, Richard Halliburton and Roy Chapman Andrews.

This is a mania that sustained me through high school and college, where I collected vintage copies of *National Geographic* and antique travel books. Then, real life and got in the way – as it usually does – and for years my yearning for the bush became something of a joke; the dream I had that died the hardest. (I'm lucky, though! Eventually I did make it into the jungles, and left my footprint in Burma, Costa Rica and Cambodia!)

*Jungle Calls* is aptly titled because the jungle has been calling me forever. As you can tell, it is really how I imagined what it would be like in the wilds of the 30s. Hero Richmond Kane is named after actor Kane Richmond, who starred as both the Shadow and a jungle explorer in *The Lost City* movie serial. The jungle gods are inspired by Robert E. Howard and H.P. Lovecraft, also young affections, and several elements of the story, like the Mannlicher, come from my nonfiction reading of the period.

My plan, in writing it, was to make it as *pulpy* as I possibly could, while hopefully throwing in a surprising supernatural twist at the end. I shot for the *rat-a-tat* staccato delivery of the period and even threw in a few contemporary jokes.

Does it work? No writer ever thinks that they pull off everything they hope to, but I hope I come close.

**BOB MADISON** - writes all kinds of stuff, including magazine articles, blogposts, television documentaries, nonfiction books, cookbooks, novels, and even ... trading cards. He grew up reading pulp reprints during the Nostalgia

Craze of 1970s, and lived on vintage comic strips, adventure novels, Classic Hollywood and Old Time Radio. For most of his boyhood, his imaginative space was somewhere in 1933. Bob wrote the narration for 2021 documentary Dark Shadows and Beyond: The Jonathan Frid Story for MPI, produced and directed by Mary O'Leary. It was nominated for a Daytime Emmy Award. His first two novels, Cash and Carrey, a comic novel, and SPIKED!, a young adult novel, were published by Vulpine Press. Bob Madison has been married since 1990, and lives in Huntington Beach, CA. Bob currently sits on the board for The Literacy Volunteers of Huntington Beach Public Library. He has also specializes in writing about himself in the Third Person. This is One of Those Times.

# EXCITING JUNGLE ACTION!

*Airship 27 Productions offers up this new antholgy brand new adventures of Ki-Gor and his lovely, red-headed mate, Helene, as they travel into the mysterious, uncharted jungles of Africa.*

Featuring a stunning cover by painter Bryan Fowler with magnificent interior illustrations by Kelly Everaert, *JUNGLE TALES Volume One* kicks off a new series pulp fans are sure to approve of happily. Penned by Aaron Smith, Duane Spurlock and W. Peter Miller, here are a trio of fast-paced tales that have the Jungle Lord discovering a hidden village of Vikings, crossing paths with dinosaurs in a lost valley and battling cannibals to save the life of a benevolent jungle princess. This is the pulse-pounding action and thrill-a-minute adventure fans have come to expect from the classic jungle pulps.

Volume Two features writer John R. Rose who offers up a trilogy of original tales; a long novella and two short stories. In this exciting volume Ki-Gor and his friends discover a hidden world, battle Nazi agents and run afoul of greedy treasure hunters. This is classic pulp jungle action reliving the days when Africa was still a vast, uncharted continent and only the bravest of the brave dared to venture within its lost and hidden realms.

www.ingramcontent.com/pod-product-compliance
Lightning Source LLC
Chambersburg PA
CBHW070822250626
47170CB00006B/2188